LINUXRULZ: Want to go to dinner at the Screening ...om?
They're showing the first *Star Wars*.

P7-EPB-884

OH, MY GOD!!!!!!!! MICHAEL *WAS* ASKING ME OUT!!!!!!!!! Dinner and a movie. At the

DATE DUE

you sit at a table and eat dinner while the movie is going. An ... ime, aft ... ckier tha ...

BOOKS BY
MEG CABOT

THE PRINCESS DIARIES

THE PRINCESS DIARIES, VOLUME II: PRINCESS IN THE SPOTLIGHT

THE PRINCESS DIARIES, VOLUME III: PRINCESS IN LOVE

THE PRINCESS DIARIES, VOLUME IV: PRINCESS IN WAITING

THE PRINCESS DIARIES, VOLUME IV AND A HALF: PROJECT PRINCESS

THE PRINCESS DIARIES, VOLUME V: PRINCESS IN PINK

THE PRINCESS DIARIES, VOLUME VI: PRINCESS IN TRAINING

THE PRINCESS PRESENT: A PRINCESS DIARIES BOOK

PRINCESS LESSONS: A PRINCESS DIARIES BOOK

PERFECT PRINCESS: A PRINCESS DIARIES BOOK

THE MEDIATOR 1: SHADOWLAND

THE MEDIATOR 2: NINTH KEY

THE MEDIATOR 3: REUNION

THE MEDIATOR 4: DARKEST HOUR

THE MEDIATOR 5: HAUNTED

THE MEDIATOR 6: TWILIGHT

ALL-AMERICAN GIRL

TEEN IDOL

NICOLA AND THE VISCOUNT

VICTORIA AND THE ROGUE

MEG CABOT

The Princess Diaries, Volume IV

Princess in Waiting

HarperTrophy®
An Imprint of HarperCollins Publishers

Harper Trophy® is a registered trademark of
HarperCollins Publishers Inc.

Princess in Waiting
Copyright © 2003 by Meggin Cabot

Library of Congress Cataloging-in-Publication Data
Cabot, Meg.
    Princess in waiting / Meg Cabot.
        p.   cm. — (The princess diaries ; v. 4)
    Summary: Princess Mia is introduced to her Genovian subjects,
and more importantly, she goes out on a date.
    ISBN 0-06-009607-1 — ISBN 0-06-009608-X (lib. bdg.)
    ISBN 0-06-009609-8 (pbk.)
    [1. Princesses—Fiction.   2. Dating (Social customs)—Fiction.]
I. Title.   II. Series.
PZ7.C11165 Pu   2003   2002151056
[Fic]—dc21   CIP
                                                              AC

Typography by Alison Donalty
❖
First Harper Trophy edition, 2004
Visit us on the World Wide Web!
www.harperteen.com

For Walter Schretzman,
and the many others who scatter largesse so
selflessly throughout New York City.
Don't think we haven't noticed.

With thanks.

ACKNOWLEDGMENTS

Many thanks to Beth Ader, Alexandra Alexo, Jennifer Brown, Kim Goad Floyd, Darcy Jacobs, Laura Langlie, Amanda Maciel, Abby McAden, and Benjamin Egnatz.

Belated thanks to the Beckham family, especially Julie, for so generously allowing me to borrow Molly's sock-swallowing habit!

"If I was a princess," she murmured, "I could scatter largess to the populace. But even if I am only a pretend princess, I can invent little things to do for people. I'll pretend that to do things for people is scattering largess."

A LITTLE PRINCESS
Frances Hodgson Burnett

MY NEW YEAR'S RESOLUTIONS
BY PRINCESS AMELIA MIGNONETTE
GRIMALDI THERMOPOLIS RENALDO,
AGE 14 YEARS AND 8 MONTHS

1. I will stop biting my fingernails, including the
   fake ones.
2. I will stop lying. Grandmère knows when I am
   lying anyway, thanks to my traitorous nostrils,
   which flare every time I tell a fib, so it's not like
   there is even a point in trying to be less than
   truthful.
3. I will never veer from prepared script while
   delivering televised address to the Genovian
   public.
4. I will stop accidentally saying *mèrde* in front of
   the ladies-in-waiting.
5. I will stop asking François, my Genovian
   bodyguard, to teach me French swear words.
6. I will apologize to the Genovian Olive Growers
   Association for that thing with the pits.
7. I will apologize to the Royal Chef for slipping
   Grandmère's dog that slice of foie gras (even
   though I have told the palace kitchen repeatedly
   that I do not eat liver).

8. I will stop lecturing the Royal Genovian Press Corps on the evils of smoking. If they all wish to develop lung cancer, that is their prerogative.
9. I will achieve self-actualization.
10. I will stop thinking so much about Michael ● Moscovitz.

Oh, wait. It's okay for me to think about Michael Moscovitz, BECAUSE HE IS MY BOYFRIEND NOW!!!!!!!!

MT + MM = TRUE LOVE 4-EVER

You know, I am supposed to be on vacation. Seriously. I mean, this is my winter break. I am supposed to be having fun, mentally recharging for the coming semester, which is not going to be easy, as I will be moving on to Algebra II, not to mention Health and Safety class. Everybody at school was all, *Oh, you are so lucky, you get to spend Christmas in a castle being waited on hand and foot.*

Well, first of all, there is nothing so great about living in a castle. Because guess what? Castles are totally old. And yeah, it's not like this one was built in 4 A.D., or whenever it was my ancestress Princess Rosagunde first became ruler of Genovia. But it was still built in, like, the 1600s, and let me tell you what they didn't have in the 1600s:

1. Cable
2. DSL
3. Toilets

Which is not to say there isn't a satellite dish now, but, hello, this is my dad's place; the only channels he has got programmed are, like, CNN, CNN Financial News, and the golf channel. Where is MTV 2, I ask you? Where is the Lifetime Movie Channel for Women?

Not that it matters because I am spending all my time being run off my feet. It isn't as if I ever even get a free moment to pick up a remote and go, "Ho hum, I wonder if there's a Tracey Gold movie on."

Oh, yeah, and the toilets? Let me just tell you that back in the 1600s, they didn't know so much about sewage. So now, four hundred years later, if you put one square too much toilet paper in the bowl and try to flush, you create a mini indoor tsunami.

So that's it. That is my life in Genovia.

Every other kid I know is spending his or her winter break in Aspen skiing, or in Miami getting tanned.

But me? What am *I* doing for my winter break?

Well, here are the highlights from the new *datebook* Grandmère gave me for Christmas (what girl wouldn't love to get a *datebook* for Christmas?) of what I have done so far:

Sunday, December 21
Royal Daily Schedule

Arrived in Genovia. Due to large bagful of Skittles consumed on flight over, almost barfed on official Genovian welcome committee who came to airport to greet me as I disembarked from the plane.

* * *

One full day since I last saw Michael. Tried calling him at his grandparents' house in Boca Raton, where the Moscovitzes have gone for winter break, but no one answered, perhaps because of time difference, Genovia being six hours ahead of Florida.

Monday, December 22
Royal Daily Schedule

While touring naval cruiser, the *Prince Phillipe*, tripped over anchor, accidentally knocking Admiral Pepin into the Genovian harbor. He was okay, though. They fished him out with a harpoon.

But why am I the only one in this country who thinks pollution is an important issue? If people are going to dock their yachts in the Genovian harbor, they really ought to pay attention to what they are throwing overboard. I mean, porpoises get their noses stuck in those plastic six-pack holders all the time, and then they starve to death because they can't open their mouths to eat. All people have to do is snip the loops before they throw the holders out, and everything would be fine.

Well, all right, not *everything*, since you shouldn't be throwing trash overboard in the first place.

I simply cannot stand idly by while helpless sea creatures are being abused by a bunch of Bain de Soleil addicts in search of that perfect Saint-Tropez tan.

Two days since last saw Michael. Tried calling him twice. First time, no answer. Second time, Michael's grandmother answered and said I had just missed him, as Michael had gone to the pharmacy to pick up his grandfather's prescription foot powder. This is so like him, always thinking of others before himself.

Tuesday, December 23
Royal Daily Schedule

At breakfast with Genovian Olive Growers Association, mentioned unseasonable drought afflicting Mediterranean area must be the "pits." No one seemed to think this joke particularly amusing, particularly members of Olive Growers Association.

Three days since last saw Michael. No time to call due to pit controversy.

Wednesday, December 24
Royal Daily Schedule

Gave televised Christmas Eve greeting to Genovian public. Strayed somewhat from prepared speech by mentioning amount of revenue generated in five boroughs of New York City by parking meters, and expressed belief that installing parking meters in Genovia would contribute greatly to national economy, while also discouraging cheapskate day-trippers from venturing across our border. Still have no idea why Grandmère was so mad about the whole thing. New York City parking meters are NOT hideously ugly blights on landscape. Most of the time, I never even notice them at all.

Four days SLSM (since last saw Michael)

Thursday, December 25, Christmas
Royal Daily Schedule

SPOKE TO MICHAEL AT LAST!!!!!! Was finally able to get through to him. Conversation somewhat stilted, however, as my father, grandmother, and cousin René were all in room from which I was calling, and Michael's parents, grandparents, and sister were in room in which he received call.

He asked me if I got anything good for Christmas, and I said no, nothing but a *datebook* and a scepter. What I wanted was a cell phone. Asked Michael if he got anything good for Hanukkah, and he said no, nothing but a color printer. Which is still better than what I got, if you ask me. Although scepter excellent for pushing back cuticles.

I am so relieved that Michael hasn't forgotten all about me. I know my boyfriend is vastly superior to all the other members of his species—guys, I mean. But everyone knows that guys are like dogs—their short-term memory is completely nil. You tell them your favorite fictional character is Xena, Warrior Princess, and next thing you know, they are going on about how your favorite fictional character is Xica of Telemundo. Boys just don't know any better, on account of how their brains are too filled up with stuff about modems and *Star Trek Voyager* and Limp Bizkit and all.

Michael is no exception to this rule. Oh, I know he

is co-valedictorian of his class and got a perfect score on his SATs and was accepted early decision to one of the most prestigious universities in the country. But you know it took him about five million years even to admit he liked me. And that was only after I'd sent him all these anonymous love letters. Which turned out not to be so anonymous because he fully knew it was me the whole time, thanks to all of my friends, including his little sister, having such exceptionally large mouths.

But whatever. I am just saying, five days is a long time to go without a word from your one true love. I mean, Tina Hakim Baba's boyfriend, Dave Farouq El-Abar, sometimes goes that long without calling her, and Tina always becomes convinced that Dave's met a girl who is better than she is. She even confronted him about it once, telling him that she loved him and that it hurt her when he didn't call . . . which only caused him not to call anymore, since Dave turns out to be commitment-phobic.

It would be very easy for Michael to meet a girl who is better than me. I mean, there must be millions of girls out there who have things actually going for them, aside from being a princess, and who don't have to spend their holidays cooped up in a palace with their crazy grandma and her freakish hairless toy poodle.

And even though when Tina starts insisting Dave's dumping her, and we all go, "Oh, he's not," I think I am starting to know how she feels.

Talked to Mom and Mr. Gianini. They are both doing fine, though my mom still won't let the doctor tell her what it is she's having—a boy or a girl. Mom says she doesn't want to know, since if it's a boy she won't push, due to not wanting to bring another Y-chromosomed oppressor into the world (Mr. G says that is just the hormones talking, but I'm not so sure. My mom can be pretty anti–Y-chromosome when she puts her mind to it). They put Fat Louie up to the phone so I could wish him a merry Christmas, and he growled with annoyance, so I know he is doing fine as well.

5 DSLSM

Friday, December 26
Royal Daily Schedule

Forced to watch father and cousin René play in charity golf tournament against Tiger Woods. Tiger won (no surprise) as Dad is middle-aged and Prince René confessed to having attended grappa-tasting party the night before. Only sport more boring than golf is polo. Going to be forced to watch Dad and cousin René play *that* next month—although technically anyway, René is barely even my cousin. He's, like, eleven hundred times removed.

And even though he is a prince, he is no longer allowed by Italian law to set foot in his native land, due to the socialists running all members of the Italian royal family out of town. Poor René's ancestral palace now belongs to a famous shoe designer, who has turned it into a resort for wealthy Americans to come for the weekend and make their own pasta and drink two-hundred-year-old balsamic vinegar.

René doesn't seem to mind, though, because here in Genovia everyone still calls him His Highness Prince René, and he is extended every privilege given a member of a royal household.

Still, just because René is four years older than me and a prince and a freshman at some French business school, doesn't mean he has the right to patronize me. I mean, I believe gambling is morally wrong, and the fact that René spends so many hours at the roulette wheel instead of utilizing his time in a more productive fashion irks me.

I mentioned this to him. It just seems to me that René needs to realize there is more to life than racing around in his Alfa Romeo, or swimming in the palace indoor pool wearing nothing but one of those little black Speedos, which are very stylish here in Europe (I asked my dad to please, for the love of all that is holy, stick to trunks, which, thankfully, he has).

And okay, René just laughed at me.

But at least I can rest easy knowing I have done

everything I can to show one extremely self-absorbed prince the error of his profligate ways.

6 DSLSM

Saturday, December 27
Royal Daily Schedule

V. depressing day, as twenty-fifth anniversary of Grand-père's death. Had to hang wreath on grave, wear black veil, etc. Veil stuck to lip gloss, could not get it off by blowing, finally had to pull it off, causing hat to be swept by wind into Genovian harbor. Prince René fished it out with the help of some friendly topless sunbathers, but hat will clearly never be the same.

7 DSLSM

Sunday, December 28
Royal Daily Schedule

Prince René was caught entertaining friendly topless sunbathers in pool house. Major ballistics from my dad, who thinks at eighteen René should be aware that he has a rep for being "Prince William of the Continent," minus the crown jewels, as René's side of the family have only name and not fortune to go with it anymore, and that those girls were only using him.

René says he doesn't mind being used in that fashion, and if *he* doesn't mind, why should Dad? This only made my dad madder, however. Should have warned René it isn't wise to antagonize Dad when vein in center of forehead is throbbing, but there was no time.

Tried calling Michael; got busy signal for four hours. He must have been online. Would have e-mailed him, but only computers in palace with Internet access in administrative offices, and doors were locked.

8 DSLSM

Monday, December 29
Royal Daily Schedule

Met with Genovian casino operators. Was discouraged by their insistence on maintaining valet parking for their patrons. Explained substantial increase in revenue generated by parking meters, but was rebuffed.

Asked Dad for own key to administrative offices, so that I can e-mail Michael whenever I want, but he rebuffed me, too, due to René having been caught in administrative offices last week, photocopying his nether region. Assured Dad I would never do something this asinine, not being homeless Speedo-wearing prince filled with testosterone, but argument clearly fell on deaf ears.

* * *

Nine days since I last saw Michael, and I think I am going INSANE!!!!!!!!!!!!!!!!!!!!

Tuesday, December 30
Royal Daily Schedule

MESSAGE FROM MICHAEL via palace phone operators. Says, *Miss you, will try to call at bonne nuit.* Asked palace operators if they are sure this is what Michael said, and they insist it was. Except this message makes no sense. *Bonne nuit* means "good night," it is not a time. Possibly there is word in Klingon that sounds like *bonne nuit*? No time to call Michael myself, however, as was ensconced all day long with Genovian Minister of Defense, learning what to do in unlikely case of military incursion by hostile enemy forces.

10 DSLSM

Posed for royal portrait. Was instructed not to move, and especially not to smile. Was very hard not to, however, as Rommel, Grandmère's toy poodle, was wandering around with one of those plastic cones around his head so he won't lick away what is left of his fur. Rommel is the only dog I know with an obsessive-compulsive disorder that is causing him to lick himself bald. The American vets all thought Rommel's hair loss was due to allergies. Then, when we got to Genovia, the Royal Vet was all, "Alors! Eet is Oh Cee Dee!"

I do not like to make fun of the plight of any four-legged creature, but Rommel was funny, the way he'd lost his peripheral vision and kept bumping into suits of armor and stuff.

Royal portrait painter says he despairs of me. Let me out early to attend palace New Year's party. Was big letdown, due to not having Michael there to kiss at midnight. Tried calling him, but Moscovitzes must have been out at some beach or pool party, as no one answered.

You know what they have a lot of in Florida? Beach and pool parties. You know who goes to beach and pool parties? Girls in bikinis. Like the girls from that movie *Blue Crush*. Like that one, Kate Bosworth, who had the one blue eye and the one brown eye and the tiny shorts. Yeah, that one. How is anyone supposed to compete against a surfer girl with one blue eye and one brown eye, I'd like to know?????

René tried to kiss me at midnight, but I told him to go kiss Grandmère instead. He'd had so much champagne, he actually did it. Grandmère hit him with a decorative swan carved from a pineapple.

11 DSLSM

Thursday, January 1
Royal Daily Schedule

GOT E-MAIL FROM MICHAEL!!!!!!! René stole key to administrative offices because he said he had to "look some things up" on Netscape (he was fully scoring people on Are You Hot or Not—I caught him) and I happened to be walking by on my way to the indoor palace pool, so I demanded to be let in. René had too big of a headache from all the champagne he drank last night to fight me on the matter.

So I got online and there was this e-mail from Michael!!!!!!!! It turns out he was NOT at a party with Kate Bosworth-like girls last night:

Mia (he wrote) sorry to have missed your call, I was at my grandparents' retirement complex's New Year's bash (they played Ricky Martin and thought they were on the cutting edge). Didn't you get my message? Well, anyway, happy New Year and I really miss you and all of that.

P.S. Are they keeping you locked in a tower over there or what? Because even prisoners get phone privileges. Am I going to have to come to Genovia and climb up your hair to get you out or something?

Has there ever BEEN a more romantic note than this? He really misses me and *all of that*! And you know what *all of that* means. Love. Right? Isn't that what *all of that* means?

Made mistake of asking René. He said a man who isn't willing to put his true feelings for a woman down on paper isn't a true man at all.

I told him it wasn't paper, just e-mail, which is different.

Isn't it?

Spent all day visiting patients at Genovian General Hospital. V. depressing, not because of patients, but because of the clown that the hospital hired to cheer up the sick children. HATE CLOWNS!!!! Clowns v. scary to me ever since I read that Stephen King book *It*, which was made into a TV movie starring that guy from *The Waltons*. It is awful the way writers can take a perfectly innocent thing like a clown and turn it into vessel of evil! Had to spend entire time in hospital dodging clown, just in case he was spawn of Satan.

12 DSLSM

And now here I am, on January 2, just sitting in on a session of the Royal Genovian Parliament, pretending to be paying attention while these really old guys in wigs go on and on about parking.

Which I realize is fully my own fault. I mean, if I had never opened my mouth about the whole parking-meter thing in the first place, none of this would be happening.

But how could they not know that if we don't charge for parking, it will just encourage more people to drive over the French and Italian borders instead of taking the train, clogging up Genovia's already very busy streets and causing yet more strain on our already deteriorating infrastructure?

And I guess I should be flattered that they are taking my suggestion so seriously. I mean, yeah, I'm the Princess of Genovia, but what do *I* know? Just because I am of royal birth and happen to be in the Gifted and Talented program at Albert Einstein High School does not mean that I am actually gifted OR talented. In fact, the opposite is true. I am clearly *not* gifted, being average in just about every category you could name, with the possible exception of foot size, in which I am somewhat over-endowed. And I have no talents to speak of. In fact, I was put into Gifted and Talented class only because I was flunking Algebra and everyone decided I needed an extra period in which to study.

So really, if you think about it, it is very kind of the members of the Genovian Parliament to listen to anything *I* have to say.

But I can't really feel very grateful to them considering that every moment I spend here is another moment I am forced to spend away from my one true love. I mean, it has been thirteen days and eighteen hours since I last saw Michael. That is nearly two weeks. And during that entire time, I have only spoken to him once by phone, due to the time difference between here and the U.S. and my UNFAIR, entirely UNREALISTIC schedule of duties. I mean, where in my grueling schedule am I supposed to find time to call my boyfriend? Where?

I am telling you, it is enough to make even a nearly fifteen-year-old girl weep, the way the fates are working against Michael and me. I have not even had time to shop for his birthday, which is in three days.

I have only been his girlfriend for thirteen days, and already I am letting him down.

Well, he will just have to get in line. According to Grandmère, who should know, I am letting everyone down: Michael, the Genovian people, my dad, her, you name it.

I really don't get it. I mean, they're only *parking meters*, for crying out loud.

Thirteen days, nineteen hours since I last saw Michael.

Saturday, January 3
Royal Daily Schedule

8 a.m.–9 a.m.
Breakfast with Genovian Olympic Equestrian Team

I really have nothing against horsey people, because horses are totally cool. But *what* does the palace kitchen staff have against ketchup? Seriously, ever since I gave up on the no dairy/egg thing, on account of I can't live without cheese and McDonald's has started treating the hens that lay the eggs for their Egg McMuffins humanely, I like nothing better than an egg-and-cheese omelet for breakfast. BUT HOW CAN I ENJOY IT WITHOUT KETCHUP???? When I come back to Genovia next time, I am fully bringing a bottle of Heinz with me.

9:30 a.m.–Noon
Dedicate new modern wing of Royal Genovian Museum of Art

Hello, I paint better than some of these dudes, and I am completely talentless. At least they put one of my mom's paintings in there (Portrait of the Artist's Daughter at Age Five Refusing to Eat Hot Dogs) so that's okay.

12:30 p.m.–2 p.m.
Lunch with Genovian ambassador to Japan
Domo arigato.

2:30 p.m.–4:30 p.m.
Sit in on meeting of Genovian Parliament
Again???? Spent entire session thinking about Michael. When Michael smiles, sometimes one corner of his mouth goes up higher than the other. Also, he has extremely nice lips. And very nice, dark eyes. Eyes that can see to the depths of my soul. I miss him so much!!!!!! This sucks. I should call Amnesty International—IT IS CRUEL AND UNUSUAL PUNISHMENT TO KEEP ME FROM THE MAN I LOVE FOR SO LONG!!!

5 p.m.–6 p.m.
Tea with Genovian Historical Society
They actually had a lot of very interesting things to say about some of my relatives. It was too bad Prince René was in Monte Carlo buying a new polo pony. He might have learned a thing or two.

7 p.m.–10 p.m.
Formal dinner with members of Genovian Trade Association
Okay, René was lucky to miss this.

14 DSLSM

I don't think I'll be able to stand this much longer.

Poem for M. M.

Across the deep blue shining sea,
is Michael, far away from me.
But he doesn't seem so far away—
though I haven't seen him for fourteen days—
because in my heart Michael stays
and there he'll beat forever always.

I can see I am going to have to work harder if I am to come up with a fitting tribute to my love.

Sunday, January 4
Royal Daily Schedule

9 a.m.–10 a.m.
Mass in Royal Genovian Chapel
I thought going to church was supposed to fill you with a sense of spiritual well-being and succor. But all I feel is sleepy.

10:30 a.m.–4 p.m.
Outing with Monaco's Royal Family, Royal Genovian Yacht
Why am I the least-tan person in Genovia? And what is up with René and the Speedos? I mean, you can totally tell he thinks he's all that. And all those girls screaming his name on the dock just encourage him. I wonder if they'd still be so crazy about him if someone told them that I caught René singing an Enrique Iglesias song in front of the mirrored wall in the Reception Room, using my scepter as a pretend microphone?

4:30 p.m.–7 p.m.
Princess lessons with Grandmère
Even in Genovia, it doesn't end. As if I don't totally get why everybody is so mad about the whole speech thing. I mean, I have already sworn I will never again veer from the prepared script while addressing

the Genovian populace. Why does sh
HARPING?

7 p.m.–10 p.m.
Formal dinner with prime minister of France and
family

René disappeared for four hours with the prime
minister's twenty-year-old daughter. They said they
just went to play roulette, but if that's true, why were
they smirking so much when they got back? If René
doesn't watch it, he is going to have a Little Prince to
look out for, sooner than he thinks.

15 DSLSM

Tried to call him twice today. Michael's grandmother answered the first time and said Michael had
gone to the computer store to buy a new toner car-
tridge. Then his dad answered and said Michael and
Lilly had gone with their grandparents to go see the
latest James Bond at the dollar cinema. Lucky
ducks!!!!!!!!!!!!!!!!!!!!!!!

9:30 a.m.–Noon
Attend ballet workshops, private performance of
Sleeping Beauty

I don't know if Lilly is right about ballet being
totally sexist. I mean, the guys have to wear tights, too.
Which is actually too much information, if you know
what I mean.

12:30 p.m.–2 p.m.
Lunch with Genovian minister of tourism

Will no one acknowledge that my parking-meter
idea has merit? Furthermore, all the foot traffic from
the day-trippers coming off the cruise ships that dock
out in the Genovian harbor is destroying some of our
most historically important bridges, such as the Pont des
Vierges (Bridge of the Virgins), so named after my
great-great-great-great-great-great-great-grandmother
Agnes, who threw herself off it rather than become a
nun like her father wanted her to be (she was all right:
the royal navy fished her out and she ended up eloping

with the ship's captain, much to the consternation of the house of Renaldo). I don't care how much of Genovia's gross national product is dependent on cruise ship day-trippers. They are ruining EVERYTHING!

2:30 p.m.–4:30 p.m.

Attend father's address to local media on importance of Genovia as a global player in today's international economy

Whatever. Could I *be* more bored? Michael! Oh, Michael! Where art thou, Michael?

5 p.m.–6 p.m.

Tea with Grandmère and fellow members of Genovian Ladies Aid Society

Spilled tea on new satin shoes that had been dyed to match tea gown.

Now they match tea.

7 p.m.–11 p.m.

Formal dinner with very famous former Soviet leader and his wife

René AWOL through most of dinner. Was found after dessert cavorting in palace garden fountain with prima ballerina from Royal Genovian ballet. Dad v. upset. Tried to soothe his frazzled nerves by making small talk with his date, Miss Czech Republic, so she would feel welcome to the family, should the occasion arise.

16 DSLSM

If this goes on much longer, I will probably develop aphasia like that girl in *Firestarter*, and start thinking my dad is a hat.

Tuesday, January 6,
Royal Quarters of the Dowager Princess

HE CALLED ME!!!!!!!!!!!!!!!!

Except that I wasn't here (as usual). I was at the Royal Genovian Opera House, watching stupid *La Boheme*, which I was enjoying until all the characters I liked DIED.

He left a message with the palace operators. The message said, *Hi.*

Hi! Michael said HI!

I tried to call him back, of course, the minute I got to a phone, but the Moscovitzes were all at Le Crabbe Shacque enjoying the Senior Citizen early bird discount . . . all except Dr. Moscovitz (Mrs.) who had to stay back at the condo due to one of her patient's needing emergency counseling (a shopaholic who was having a relapse due to all the post-holiday sales).

Dr. Moscovitz said she would be sure to give Michael the message that I'd called him back. The message was: *Hi.*

Well, I wanted to say something more romantic, but it is really hard to say the word love to your boyfriend's mother, it turns out.

Oh, my God, Grandmère is yelling at me again. She has been lecturing me all day about this stupid ball that's coming up—my farewell-for-now ball, the one they're holding the night before I leave to go back to America . . . and to my love.

The thing is, Prince William is going to be at the ball, because he's going to be in Genovia anyway for the charity polo match my dad and René are playing in, and Grandmère is all worried I am going to make the same kind of social gaffe in front of Prince Wills that I made during my televised introduction to the Genovian people.

Like I am really going to stand there and talk about parking meters with Prince William. But whatever.

"I swear I do not know what is wrong with you," Grandmère is saying. "Your head has been in the clouds ever since we left New York. Even more so than usual." She is narrowing her eyes at me—always a very scary thing, because Grandmère had black kohl tattooed all around her lids so that she could spend her mornings shaving off her eyebrows and drawing new ones on rather than messing around with mascara and eyeliner. "You are not thinking about *that boy*, are you?"

That boy is what Grandmère has started calling Michael, ever since I announced that he was my reason for living. Well, except for my cat, Fat Louie, of course.

"If you are speaking of Michael Moscovitz," I just replied to her, in my most regal voice, "I most certainly am. He is never far from my thoughts, because he is my heart's breath."

Grandmère's response to this is a snort.

"Puppy love," she says. "You'll get over it soon enough."

Um, I beg your pardon, Grandmère, but I so fully will not. I have loved Michael for approximately eight years, except perhaps for a brief two-week period of time when I thought I was in love with Josh Richter. Eight years is more than half my life. A deep and abiding passion such as this cannot be dismissed as easily as that, nor can it be defined by your pedestrian grasp of human emotion.

I didn't say any of that out loud, though, on account of how Grandmère has those really sharp nails that she tends to "accidentally" poke people with.

Except that even though Michael really is my reason for living and my heart's breath, I don't think I'll be decorating my Algebra notebook with hearts and flowers and curlicue *Mrs. Michael Moscovitz*es, the way Lana Weinberger decorated hers (only with *Mrs. Josh Richter*s, of course). Not only because doing stuff like that is completely lame and because I do not care to have my identity subjugated by taking my husband's name, but also because as consort to the regent of Genovia, Michael will of course have to take my name. Not Thermopolis. Renaldo. Michael Renaldo. That looks kind of nice, now that I think about it.

Thirteen more days until I see the lights of New

York and Michael's dark brown eyes again. Please
God, let me live that long.

HRH Michael Renaldo
    M. Renaldo, prince consort
        Michael Moscovitz Renaldo of Genovia

Seventeen days since I last saw Michael.

All I have to say about today is that if these people WANT their infrastructure to be destroyed by gas-guzzling sports utility vehicles driven by German tourists, that is entirely their prerogative. Who am I to try to stand in their way?

Oh, I'm sorry, just their PRINCESS.

18 DSLSM

Thursday, January 8
Royal Daily Schedule

8 a.m.–9 a.m.
Breakfast with ambassador to Spain
Still no ketchup!!!

9:30 a.m.–Noon
Final touch-ups to royal portrait
I am not allowed to see finished product until unveiling at Farewell Ball. Hope artist did not include large zit I have begun sprouting on chin. That could be kind of embarrassing.

12:30 p.m.–2 p.m.
Lunch with Genovian minister of finance
FINALLY! Someone who agrees with me on fiscal importance of parking meters. Minister of finance is *the man!*

Sadly, Grandmère still not convinced. And she, far more than Dad or Parliament, is the one with the most influence over public opinion.

2:30 p.m.–4:30 p.m.
More coaching on what is okay versus not okay to say to Prince William when I meet him

Example:

"I am very pleased to make your acquaintance."
—Okay

"Has anyone ever told you that you look like Heath Ledger?" —Not okay

René strolled by in the middle of my coaching session on his way to the palace weight room and suggested that I ask Wills what really happened between him and Britney Spears. Grandmère says that if I do, she will leave Rommel in my care next time she goes to Baden-Baden to get a face peel. Ew! to both taking care of Rommel *and* the face peel. And to René, too, for that matter.

7 p.m.–11 p.m.
Formal dinner with largest import/exporter of Genovian olive oil
Whatever.

19 DSLSM

This just occurred to me:

When Michael said he loved me that night during the Nondenominational Winter Dance, he might have meant love in the platonic sense. Not love in the tides of flaming passion sense. You know, like, maybe he loves me like a friend.

Only you don't generally stick your tongue in your friend's mouth, do you?

Well, maybe here in Europe you might. But not in America, for God's sake.

Except Josh Richter used tongue that time he kissed me in front of the school, and he was certainly never in love with me!!!!!!!!!!

This is very upsetting. Seriously. I realize it is the middle of the night and I should be at least trying to sleep since tomorrow I have to cut the ribbon at the new Royal Genovian Foundling Home.

But how can I sleep when my boyfriend could be in Florida loving me as a friend and possibly at this very minute actually falling in love with Kate Bosworth? I mean, unlike me, Kate is actually good at something (surfing). Kate belongs in Gifted and Talented, *not me*.

Why am I so stupid? Why didn't I demand that Michael specify when he said he loved me? Why didn't I go, "Love me how? Like a friend? Or like a life partner?"

I am such an idiot.

I am never going to be able to sleep now. I mean, how can I, knowing that the man I love could conceivably think of me only as a friend he likes to French kiss?

There is just one thing I can do: I have to call the only person I know who might be able to help me. And it is okay to call her because

1. it is only seven o'clock where she is, and

2. she got her own cell phone for Christmas, so even though right now she is skiing in Aspen, I can still reach her, even if she is on a ski lift, or whatever.

Thank God I have my own phone in my room. Even though I *do* have to dial 9 to get a line outside of the palace.

20 DSLSM

Tina answered on the very first ring! She totally wasn't on a ski lift. She sprained her ankle on a slope yesterday. Oh, thank you, God, for causing Tina to sprain her ankle, so that she could be there for me in my hour of need.

And it is okay, because she says it only hurts when she moves.

Tina was in her room at the ski lodge, watching the Lifetime Movie Channel when I called (*Co-ed Call Girl*, in which Tori Spelling portrays a young woman struggling to pay for her college education with money earned working as an escort—based on a true story).

At first it was very difficult to get Tina to focus on the situation at hand. All she wanted to know about was what I'm going to say when I meet Prince William. I tried to explain to her that according to Grandmère, I am not allowed to say anything to Prince William beyond *It is very nice to meet you*. She is apparently fearful that I will launch into my treatise on parking meters, which she finds less than scintillating.

Besides, what does it even matter what I say to him? My heart belongs to another.

This response was extremely dissatisfying to Tina.

"The least you can do," she said, "is get his e-mail address for me. I mean, not everyone is in as an emotionally satisfying romantic relationship as you are, Mia."

Ever since she started going out with him, Tina's boyfriend, Dave, has shied away from commitment, saying that a man can't let himself get tied down before the age of sixteen. So even though Tina claims Dave is her Romeo in cargo pants, she has been keeping her eyes open for a nice boy willing to make a commitment. Although I think Prince William is too old for her. I suggested she try for Will's little brother, Harry, who I hear is actually very cute as well, but Tina said then she'd never get to be queen, a sentiment I guess I can understand, although believe me, being royal loses a lot of its glamour once it actually happens to you.

"Okay," I said. "I'll do my best to get Prince William's e-mail address for you. But I do have other things on my mind, Tina. Like for instance that there is a distinct possibility that Michael only likes me as a friend."

"What?" Tina was shocked. "But I thought you said he used the L word the night of the Non-denominational Winter Dance!"

"He did," I said. "Only he didn't say he was *in* love with me. He just said he loved me."

Fortunately I didn't have to explain any further. Tina has read enough romance novels to know exactly what I was getting at.

"Guys don't say the word *love* unless they mean it,

Mia," she said. "I *know*. Dave never uses it with me."
There was a throb of pain in her voice.

"Yes, I know," I said, sympathetically. "But the
question is, *how* did Michael mean it? I mean, Tina,
I've heard him say he loves his dog. But he is not *in* love
with his dog."

"I guess I can see what you mean," Tina said,
though she sounded kind of doubtful. "So, what are you
going to do?"

"That's why I called you!" I said. "I mean, do you
think I should just ask him?"

Tina let out a cry of pain. I thought it was because
she'd jiggled her sprained ankle, but really it was
because she was so horrified by what I'd asked.

"Of course you can't just come out and ask him!"
she cried. "You can't put him on the spot like that.
You've got to be more subtle. Remember, he's Michael,
which of course makes him vastly superior to most
guys . . . but he's still a guy."

I hadn't thought of this. I hadn't thought of a lot of
things, apparently. I couldn't believe that I had just
been going along on this sea of bliss, happy just to
know Michael even liked me, while the whole time, he
could have been falling in love with some other, more
intellectually or athletically gifted girl.

"Well," I said. "Maybe I should just be like, 'Do
you like me as a friend, or do you like me as a girlfriend?'"

"Mia," Tina said. "I really do not think you should ask Michael point-blank like that. He might run away in fear, like a startled fawn. Boys have a tendency to do that, you know. They aren't like us. They don't like to talk about their feelings."

It is just so sad that to get any kind of trustworthy advice about men, I have to call someone eight thousand miles away. Thank God for Tina Hakim Baba, is all I have to say.

"So what do you think I should do?" I asked.

"Well, it's going to be hard for you to do anything," Tina said, "until you get back here. The only way to tell what a boy is feeling is to look into his eyes. You'll never get anything out of him over the phone. Boys are no good at talking on the phone."

This was certainly true, if my ex-boyfriend Kenny had been any sort of indication.

"I know," Tina said, sounding like she'd just gotten a good idea. "Why don't you ask Lilly?"

"I don't know," I said. "I'd feel kind of funny about dragging her into something that's between Michael and me—" The truth was, Lilly and I still hadn't really even talked about me liking her brother, and her brother liking me back. I had always thought she'd be kind of mad about it. But then it turned out in the end she actually kind of helped us get together, by telling Michael I was the one who'd been sending him those anonymous love letters.

"Just ask her," Tina said.

"But it's really late there," I said.

"Late? It's only, like, nine o'clock in Florida!"

"Yeah, and that's what time Lilly and Michael's grandparents go to bed. I don't want to call and wake them up. Then they'll hate me forever." _And it will make things uncomfortable at the wedding._ I didn't say this part out loud. Although probably I could have, and Tina would have understood.

"They won't care if you wake them up, Mia," Tina said. "You're calling from a different time zone. They'll understand. And be sure to call me back after you talk to her! I want to know what she says."

I have to admit that, as I dialed, my fingers were shaking. Not so much because I was afraid of waking up Mr. and Mrs. Moscovitz and having them hate me for it forever, but because there was a chance Michael might answer. What was I going to say if he did? I had no idea. The only thing I knew for sure was that I was not going to say, "Do you like me as a friend, or do you like me as a girlfriend?" Because Tina had told me not to.

Lilly answered on the first ring. Our conversation went like this:

Lilly: Whoa. It's you.

Me: Is it too late to call? I didn't wake up
           your grandparents, did I?

Lilly:	Well, yeah. Kinda. But they'll get over it. So. How is it?
Me:	You mean Genovia? Um, okay, I guess.
Lilly:	Oh, yes. I'm sure it's just okay, being waited on hand and foot, having your every need tended to by servants, and wearing a crown all the time.
Me:	The crown kind of hurts. Look. Just tell me the truth, Lilly. Has Michael found another girl?
Lilly:	Another girl? What are you talking about?
Me:	You know what I mean. Some Floridian girl, who can surf. Some girl named Kate, or possibly Anne Marie, with one blue eye and one brown eye. Just tell me, Lilly, I can take the truth, I swear.
Lilly:	First of all, for Michael to have met another girl, that would mean he'd have to tear himself from his laptop and leave the condo, which he has done only for meals and to buy more computer

equipment the entire time we have been here. He is as pasty-skinned as ever. Secondly, he is not going to go out with some girl named Kate, because he likes *you*.

Me: (practically crying with relief) Really, Lilly? You swear? You aren't just lying to make me feel better?

Lilly: No, I'm not. Though I don't know how long his devotion to you is going to last, considering you didn't even remember his birthday.

I felt something clutch at my throat. Michael's birthday! I had forgotten Michael's birthday! I had written it in my new datebook and everything, but with everything that had been going on . . .

"Oh, my God, Lilly," I shrieked. "I completely forgot!"

"Yes," Lilly said. "You did. But don't worry. I'm pretty sure he didn't expect a card or anything. I mean, you're off being the Princess of Genovia. How can you be expected to remember something as important as your boyfriend's birthday?"

This seemed really unfair to me. I mean, Michael and I have only been going out for twenty-two days, and for twenty-one of them, I have been very, very busy. I mean, it is all very well for Lilly to joke, but I haven't seen her christening any battleships or crusading for the installation of public parking meters. It may never have occurred to anyone, but this princess stuff is hard work.

"Lilly," I said. "Can I talk to him, please? Michael, I mean?"

"Sure," Lilly said. Then she screamed, "Michael! Phone!"

"Lilly!" I cried, shocked. "Your grandparents!"

"Puh-*lease*," she said. "This'll get them back for slamming the front door at five every single morning when they go to pick up the *Times*."

It was a long time after that that I finally heard some footsteps, and then Michael going to Lilly, "Thanks." Then Michael picked up the phone and went, kind of curiously, since Lilly hadn't told him who it was, "Hello?"

Just hearing his voice made me forget all about how it was after three in the morning and I was miserable and hating my life. Suddenly it was like it was two in the afternoon and I was lying on one of the beaches I was working so hard to protect from erosion and pollution by tourists, with the warm sun pouring down on me and someone offering me an ice-cold Orangina from a silver tray. That's how Michael's voice made me feel.

"Michael," I said. "It's me."

"Mia," he said, sounding genuinely happy to hear from me. I don't think it was my imagination, either. He really did sound pleased, and not like he was getting ready to dump me for Kate Bosworth at all. "How are you?"

"I'm okay," I said. Then, to get it out as soon as possible, I went, "Listen, Michael, I can't believe I missed your birthday. I suck. I can't believe how much I suck. I am the most horrible person who ever walked the face of the planet."

Then Michael did a miraculous thing. He laughed. Laughed! Like missing his birthday was nothing!

"Oh, that's all right," he said. "I know you're busy over there. And there's that time-zone thing, and all. So. How's it going? Has your grandmother let you off for that parking-meter thing, or is she still on your case about it?"

I practically melted right there in the middle of my big, fancy royal bed, with the phone clutched to my ear and everything. I couldn't believe he was being so nice to me, after the terrible thing I had done. It wasn't like twenty days had gone by at all. It was like we were still standing in front of my stoop, with the snow coming down and looking so white against Michael's dark hair and Lars getting mad in the vestibule because we wouldn't stop kissing and he was cold and wanted to go inside already.

I couldn't believe I had ever thought Michael might

fall in love with some Floridian girl with multicolored eyes and a surfboard. I mean, I still wasn't exactly sure he was in love with me, or anything. But I was pretty sure he *liked* me.

And right there, at three in the morning, sitting by myself in my royal bedchamber in the Palais de Genovia, that was enough.

So then I asked him about his birthday, and he told me how they'd gone to Red Lobster and Lilly'd had an allergic reaction to her shrimp cocktail and they'd had to cut the meal short to go to Promptcare because she'd swollen up like Violet in *Willy Wonka and the Chocolate Factory*, and now she has to carry a syringe filled with adrenaline around with her in case she accidentally ingests shellfish ever again, and how Michael's parents got him a new laptop for when he goes to college and how when he gets back to New York he is thinking about starting a band since he is having trouble finding sponsors for his webzine *Crackhead* on account of how he did that groundbreaking exposé on how much Windows sucks and how he only uses Linux now.

Apparently a lot of *Crackhead*'s former subscribers are frightened of the wrath of Bill Gates and his minions.

I was so happy to be listening to Michael's voice that I didn't even notice what time it was or how sleepy I was getting until he went, "Hey, isn't it, like, four in the morning there?" which by that point it was. Only

I didn't care because I was so happy just to be talking to him.

"Yes," I said dreamily.

"Well, you'd better get to bed," Michael said. "Unless you get to sleep in. But I bet you have stuff to do tomorrow, right?"

"Oh," I said, still all lost in rhapsody, which is what the sound of Michael's voice sends me into. "Just a ribbon-cutting ceremony at the hospital. And then lunch with the Genovian Historical Society. And then a tour of the Genovian zoo. And then dinner with the minister of culture and his wife."

"Oh, my God," Michael said, sounding alarmed. "Do you have to do that kind of stuff every day?"

"Uh-huh," I said, wishing I was there with him, so that I could gaze into his adorably brown eyes while hearing his adorably deep voice, and thus know whether or not he loved me, since this was, according to Tina, the only way you could tell with boys.

"Mia," he said, with some urgency. "You'd better get some sleep. You have another huge day ahead of you."

"Okay," I said happily.

"I mean it, Mia," he said. He can be so authoritative sometimes, just like the Beast in *Beauty and the Beast*, my favorite movie of all time. Or the way Patrick Swayze bosses Baby around in *Dirty Dancing*. So, so exciting. "Hang up the phone and go to bed."

"You hang up first," I said.

Sadly, he got less bossy after this. Instead, he started talking in this voice I had only ever heard him use once before, and that was on the stoop in front of my mom's apartment building the night of the Nondenominational Winter Dance, when we did all that kissing.

Which was actually even more exhilarating than when he was bossing me around, to be truthful.

"No," he said. "You hang up first."

"No," I said, thrilled to pieces. "You."

"No," he said. "You."

"Both of you hang up," Lilly said, very rudely, over the extension. "I have to call Boris before his nightly Benadryl kicks in."

So we both said good-bye very hastily and hung up.

But I'm almost positive Michael would have said I love you if Lilly hadn't been on the line.

Ten days until I see him again. I can hardly WAIT!!!!!!!!

Saturday, January 10
Royal Daily Schedule

1 p.m. – 3 p.m.

Lunch with Genovian Historical Society

Grandmère can be so mean. Seriously. Imagine pinching me, just because she thought I had dozed off for a few seconds at lunch! I swear I am going to have a bruise now. It's a good thing I don't have any time to go to the beach, because if I did and anyone saw the mark she'd left, they'd probably call Genovian Child Protective Services, or whatever.

And I wasn't asleep, either. I was just resting my eyes.

Grandmère says it is thoughtless of "that boy" to keep me up all hours whispering sweet nothings in my ear. She says Prince René would never treat any of his girlfriends so cavalierly.

I informed her very firmly that Michael had actually *told* me to hang up, because he cares very deeply about me, and that *I* was the one who kept on talking. And that we don't whisper sweet nothings to each other, we have substantive discussions about art and literature and Bill Gates's stranglehold on the software industry.

To which Grandmère replied, *"Pfuit!"*

But you can tell she is totally jealous because she would like a boyfriend who is as smart and thoughtful as mine. But that will so never happen, because Grandmère is too mean, and besides, there is that whole thing she does with her eyebrows. Boys like girls with real eyebrows, not painted-on ones.

Nine days until I am once more in the arms of my love.

Saturday, January 10, 11 p.m.,
Royal Genovian bedchamber

I am so excited! Tina, not being able to join her family on the ski slopes, spent all day in an Aspen Internet café looking up all of her friend's horoscopes. Last night she faxed over me and Michael's horoscopes! I am taping them here in my datebook so I won't lose them. They are so accurate it is making my spine tingle.

Michael—Date of Birth = January 5

Capricorn is the leader of the Earth signs. Here is a stabilizing force, one of the hardest-working signs of the Zodiac. The Mountain Goat has intense powers of self-concentration, but not in an egotistical sense. Members of this sign find a great deal more confidence in what they do than in who they are. Capricorn is one very high achiever! Without balance, however, Capricorn can become too rigid, and focus too much on achievement. Then they forget the little joys in life. When the Goat finally relaxes and enjoys life, his or her most delightful secrets emerge. No one has a better sense of humor than the Capricorn. Oh, that Cap might let us bask in that warm smile!

Mia—Date of Birth = May 1

Ruled by loving Venus, Taurus has great emotional

depth. Friends and lovers rely on the warmth and emotional accessibility of the Bull. Taurus represents consistency, loyalty, and patience. Fixed earth can be very rigid, too cautious to take some of the risks necessary in life. Sometimes the Bull ends up temporarily stuck in the mud. He or she may not want to rise to every challenge or potential. And stubborn? Yes! The Taurean Bull may always surface. This sign's Yin energy can also go too far, causing Taurus to become very, very passive. Still, you cannot ask for a better lover or more loyal friend.

Michael + Mia

Courageous, ambitious Earth signs, Taurus and Capricorn seem to be made for each other. Both value career success and share a love of beauty and of lasting, classical foundations. Capricorn's irony charms the Bull, while the latter's expert sensuality rescues the Goat from his or her obsession with career. They enjoy talking together, and communication is excellent. They confide in each other, one promising never to offend or betray the other. This could be a perfect couple.

See? We're perfect for each other! But expert sensuality? *Me?* Um, I don't think so.

Still . . . I'm so happy! Perfect! You can't get better than perfect!

Sunday, January 11
Royal Daily Schedule

9 a.m.–10 a.m.
Mass in Royal Genovian Chapel

Oh, my God, I have only been Michael's girlfriend for twenty-four days, and already I'm terrible at it. The girlfriend thing, I mean. I can't even figure out what to get him for his birthday. He is the love of my life, the reason my heart beats. You would think I would know what to get the guy.

But no. I haven't got a clue.

Tina says the only appropriate thing to get for a boy you have only been officially dating for less than four weeks is a sweater. And she says even that is pushing it, since Michael and I have not even been out on an official date yet—so technically, how can we be dating?

But a *sweater*? I mean, that is so unromantic. That is the kind of thing I would get my dad—if he wasn't so in need of anger management manuals, which is what I got for him for Christmas. I would get a sweater for my stepdad for sure.

But my *boyfriend*?

I was kind of surprised Tina would suggest something so banal, as she is basically the resident romance expert of our little group. But Tina says the rules about what to give boys are actually very strict. Her mom told them to her. Tina's mom used to be a model and international jet-setter who once dated a sultan, so I guess she would know. The rules for presents for guys, according to Mrs. Hakim Baba, go:

Length of Time Going Out:	Appropriate Gift:
1–4 months	Sweater
5–8 months	Cologne
9–12 months	Cigarette lighter*
1 year +	Watch

But this is better at least than Grandmère's list of what is appropriate to give boyfriends, which she presented to me yesterday, as soon as I mentioned to her my horrible faux pas of missing Michael's birthday. Her list goes:

Length of Time Going Out:	Appropriate Gift:
1–4 months	Candy
5–8 months	Book
9–12 months	Handkerchief
1 year +	Gloves

Handkerchiefs? Who gives handkerchiefs anymore? Handkerchiefs are completely unhygienic!

And candy? For a *guy*????

But Grandmère says the same rules apply for girls as for boys. Michael is not allowed to give me anything

---

*Mrs. Hakim Baba says that for a nonsmoker, an engraved pocketknife or brandy flask may be substituted. Whatever. Like I would ever go out with a smoker, a drinker, or someone who went around with a knife in his pocket. Ooooh, dream date!

but candy or possibly flowers for my birthday, either!

Overall, I think I prefer Mrs. Hakim Baba's list.

Still, this whole dating/present-giving thing is so difficult! Everybody says something different. Like, last night I called my mom and asked her what I should give Michael, and she said silk boxer shorts.

But I can't give Michael UNDERWEAR!!!!!!!

I wish my mom would hurry up and have this baby already so she would stop acting so weird. She is pretty much useless to me in her current state of hormonal imbalance.

Out of desperation, I asked my dad what I should get Michael, and he said a pen, so Michael could write to me while I am in Genovia, instead of my calling him all the time and breaking the bank of Genovia.

Whatever, Dad. Like anyone writes with a pen anymore.

And hello, I am only going to be in Genovia for Christmas and summers, as per our agreement drawn up last September.

A pen. I am so sure. Am I the only person in my family with a modicum of romance in my bones?

Oops, gotta stop writing, Father Christoff is looking this way. But it is his own fault. I wouldn't write in my journal during mass if his sermons were even semi-inspiring. Or at least in English.

12 p.m.–2 p.m.

Lunch with Director of Royal Genovian Opera, leading mezzo-soprano

I thought *I* was a picky eater, but it turns out mezzo-sopranos are way pickier than even princesses.

My zit is growing out of all proportion despite application of toothpaste last night before I went to bed.

3 p.m.–5 p.m.

Meeting with Genovian Homeowners Association

You would think that the Homeowners Association, at least, would be on my side on the parking meter issue. After all, it's *their* houses these tourists keep parking in front of. You'd think they'd want to bring in a little more income for sidewalk repairs. But NOOOOOOOOOOO.

I swear I don't know how my dad does this every day. I really don't.

7 p.m.–10 p.m.

Formal Dinner with ambassador to Chile and his wife

Huge controversy due to René "borrowing" Chilean ambassador's convertible Porsche—and his wife—for a jaunt into Monte Carlo after dessert. Couple eventually found playing tennis on royal court.

Sadly, it was strip tennis.

Eight days until I see him again. Oh, joy! Oh, rapture!

Monday, January 12, 1 a.m., Royal Genovian bedchamber

I just got off the phone with Michael. I *had* to call him. It wasn't like I had a choice. I had to find out what he wanted for his birthday. I know that is cheating—*asking* someone what they want—but I seriously can't think what to get him. Of course if I were the Kate Bosworth type I would so totally have gotten him the perfect gift already, like maybe a charming friendship bracelet that I wove myself out of seaweed or whatever.

But I am not Kate Bosworth. I do not even know how to weave. OH, MY GOD, I DON'T EVEN KNOW HOW TO WEAVE!!!!!!!!!!

I *have* to get him something *really* good, since I forgot. About his birthday, and all. And then of course there's the whole thing about how he is saddled with a talentless freak princess for a girlfriend, instead of a hot Kate Bosworth type who can surf and weave and is self-actualized and never gets zits and everything. I have to get him something that is so fabulous that he forgets that I am nothing but a non-surfing, fingernail-biting freshman who happened to have been born royal.

Of course Michael says he doesn't want anything, that I am the only thing he needs (if only I could believe this!!!!!!!!!!) and that he will see me in eight days, and that is the best present anyone could get him.

This seems to indicate that he might actually be in

love with me, as opposed to only loving me as a friend. I will of course have to check with Tina to see what she thinks, but I would have to say that in this case, Signs Point to Yes!

But of course he is only saying that. That he doesn't want anything for his birthday, I mean. I have to get him *something*. Something really good. Only what?

Anyway, I really did have a reason to call him. I didn't do it just because I wanted to hear the sound of his voice, or anything. I mean, I am *not* that far gone.

Oh, all right, maybe I am. How can I help it? I have only been in love with Michael since, like, forever. I love the way he says my name. I love the way he laughs. I love the way he asks my opinion, like he really cares what I think (God knows nobody around here feels that way. I mean, make a suggestion—like, that it might save water to turn off the fountain in front of the palace at night, when no one is around anyway—and everybody practically acts like one of the suits of armor in the Grand Hall started talking).

Well, okay, not my dad. But I see him less here in Genovia than I do back home, practically, because he is so caught up in parliamentary meetings and racing his yacht in regattas and hanging out with Miss Czech Republic.

Anyway, I like talking to Michael. Is that so wrong? I mean, he *is* my boyfriend, after all.

If only I were worthier of him! I mean, between my

not having remembered his birthday, my not being able to figure out what to get him, and my not really being that good at anything, the way he is, it's a wonder he's even interested in me at all!

So we were just saying good-bye after having had a perfectly pleasant conversation about the Genovian Olive Growers Association and Michael's band that he is trying to put together (he is so talented!), and whether it is off-putting to call a band Frontal Lobotomy, and I was just working up the guts to go, "I miss you," or "I love you," thus leaving an opening for him to say something similar back to me and therefore resolve the does-he-just-love-me-like-a-friend-or-is-he-in-love-with-me dilemma once and for all, when I heard Lilly in the background, demanding to talk to me.

Michael went, "Get away," but Lilly kept on shrieking, "I have to talk to her, I just remembered I have something really important to ask her."

Then Michael went, "Don't tell her about that," and my heart skipped a beat because I thought Lilly had all of a sudden remembered that Michael had been going out with some girl named Anne Marie behind my back after all. Before I could say another word, Lilly had wrestled the phone away from him (I heard Michael grunt, I guess in pain because she must have kicked him or something), and then she was going, "Oh, my God, I forgot to ask. Did you see it?"

"Lilly," I said, since even eight thousand miles away,

I could feel Michael's pain—Lilly kicks hard. I know, because I have been the recipient of quite a few kicks of hers over the years. "I know that you are used to having me all to yourself, but you are going to have to learn to share me with your brother. Now, if this means we are going to have to set boundaries in our relationship, then I guess we will have to. But you can't just go around ripping the phone out of Michael's hand when he might have had something really important to—"

"Shut up about my sainted brother for a minute. Did . . . you . . . see . . . it?"

"See what? What are you talking about?" I thought maybe somebody had tried to jump into the polar bear cage at the Central Park Zoo again.

"Oh, just the movie," Lilly said. "Of your life. The one that was on TV the other night. Or hadn't you heard your life story has been made into a movie of the week?"

I wasn't very surprised to hear this. I had already been warned that a TV movie about my life was in the works. But I'd been assured by the palace publicity staff that the movie wouldn't be shown until February sweeps. I guess the joke was on us.

Whatever. There are already four unauthorized biographies about me floating around out there. One of them made the best-seller list for about half a second. I read it. It wasn't that good. But maybe that's just because I already knew how it all turned out.

"So?" I said. I was kind of mad at Lilly. I mean, she'd booted Michael off the phone just to tell me about some dumb movie?

"Hello," Lilly said. "Movie. Of your life. You were portrayed as shy and awkward."

"I *am* shy and awkward," I reminded her.

"They made your grandmother all kindly and sympathetic to your plight," Lilly said. "It was the grossest mischaracterization I've seen since *Shakespeare in Love* tried to pass off the Bard as a hottie with a six-pack and a full set of teeth."

"That's horrible," I said. "Now can I please finish talking to Michael?"

"You didn't even ask how they portrayed *me*," Lilly said, accusingly, "your loyal best friend."

"How did they portray you, Lilly?" I asked, looking at the big fancy clock on top of the big fancy marble mantelpiece over my big fancy bedroom fireplace. "And make it quick, I've got a breakfast and then a ride with the Genovian Equestrian Society in exactly seven hours."

"They portrayed me as less than fully supportive of your royalness," Lilly practically screamed into the phone. "They made out like after you first got that stupid haircut, I mocked you for being shallow and a trend-follower!"

"Yeah," I said, waiting for her to get to the point of her tirade. Because of course Lilly hadn't been very supportive of my haircut, or my royalness.

But it turned out Lilly had already gotten to the point of her tirade.

"I was never unsupportive of your royalness!" she shrieked into the phone, causing me to hold the receiver away from my head in order to keep my eardrums intact. "I was your number-one most supportive friend through the whole thing!"

This was so patently untrue, I thought Lilly was joking, and I started to laugh. But then I realized when she greeted my laughter with stone cold silence that she was totally serious. Apparently Lilly has one of those selective memories, where she can remember all the good things she did, but none of the bad things. Kind of like a politician.

Because of course if it were true that Lilly had been so supportive of me, I never would have become friends with Tina Hakim Baba, who I only started sitting with at lunch back in October because Lilly wasn't speaking to me on account of the whole princess thing.

"I sincerely hope," Lilly said, "that you are laughing in disbelief over the idea that I was ever anything less than a good friend to you, Mia. I know we've had our ups and downs, but any time I was ever hard on you, it was only because I thought you weren't being true to yourself."

"Um," I said. "Okay."

"I am going to write a letter," Lilly went on, "to the

studio that produced that piece of libelous trash, demanding a written apology for their irresponsible screenwriting. And if they do not provide one—and publish it in a full-page ad in *Variety*—I will sue. I don't care if I have to take my case to the Supreme Court. Those Hollywood types think they can throw anything they want to in front of a camera and the viewing public will just lap it up. Well, that might be true for the rest of the proles, but *I* am going to fight for more honest portrayals of actual people and events. The man is not going to keep *me* down!"

I asked Lilly what man, thinking she meant the director or something, and she just went, "The man! The man!" like I was mentally challenged, or something.

Then Michael got back on the phone and explained that "the man" is a figurative allusion to authority, and that in the way that Freudian analysts blame everything on "the mother," blues musicians have historically blamed their woes on "the man." Traditionally, Michael informed me, "the man" is usually white, financially successful, middle-aged, and in a position of considerable power over others.

We discussed calling Michael's band The Man, but then dismissed it as having possibly misogynistic undertones.

Seven days until I can once again be in Michael's

arms. Oh, that the hours would fly as fleetly as winged doves!

I just realized—Michael's description of "The Man" sounds a lot like my dad! Although I doubt all those blues musicians were talking about the Prince of Genovia. As far as I know, my dad has never even been to Memphis.

8 p.m.–12 a.m.
Royal Genovian Symphony

Just when it seems like maybe, just maybe, things might be starting to go my way, something always has to come along to ruin it.

And as usual, it was Grandmère.

I guess she could tell because I was so sleepy again today that I'd been up all night talking to Michael. So this morning between my ride with the Equestrian Society and my meeting with the Genovian Beachfront Development Society, Grandmère sat me down and gave me a lecture. This time it wasn't about the socially acceptable gifts to give a boy on his birthday. Instead, it was about Appropriate Choices.

"It is all very well and good, Amelia," Grandmère said, "for you to like *that boy*."

"I should think so!" I cried, with righteous indignation. "Considering you have never even met him! I mean, what do you even know about Michael, anyway? Nothing!"

Grandmère just gave me the evil eye. "Nevertheless," she went on. "I do not think it wise of you to allow your affection for this Michael fellow to blind you to other, more suitable consorts, such as—"

I interrupted to tell Grandmère that if she said the

words *Prince William* I was going to jump off the Pont des Vierges.

Grandmère told me not to be more ridiculous than I already am, that I could never marry Prince William anyway, on account of his being Church of England. However, there are apparently other, infinitely more suitable romantic partners for a princess of the royal house of Renaldo than Michael. And Grandmère said she would hate for me to miss the opportunity to get to know these other young men just because I fancy myself in love with Michael. She assured me that, were the circumstances reversed, and Michael were the heir to a throne and a considerable fortune, she highly doubted he would be as scrupulously faithful as I was being.

I objected to this assessment of Michael's character very much. I informed Grandmère that, if she had ever bothered to get to know Michael, she'd have realized that in every aspect of his life, from his being editor in chief of the now defunct *Crackhead* to his role as treasurer in the Computer Club, he has shown nothing but the utmost loyalty and integrity. I also explained, as patiently as I could, that it hurt me to hear her saying anything negative about a man to whom I have pledged my heart.

"That is just it, Amelia," Grandmère said, rolling her scary eyes. "You are entirely too young to pledge your heart to anyone. I think it very unwise of you, at the age of fourteen, to decide who you are going to spend the rest of your life with. Unless, of course, it happened to be someone very, very special. Someone your father and I know. *Very, very* well. Someone who, while possibly *seeming* a bit immature, probably just needs the right woman to make him settle down. Girls mature much more quickly than young men, Amelia—"

I interrupted Grandmère to inform her that I will be fifteen in four months, and also that Juliet was fourteen when she married Romeo. To which Grandmère replied, "And that relationship turned out very nicely, didn't it!"

Grandmère clearly has never been in love. Furthermore, she has no appreciation whatsoever for romantic tragedy.

"And in any case," Grandmère added, "if you hope to keep *that boy*, you are going about it all wrong."

I thought it was very unsupportive of Grandmère to be suggesting that I, after only having had a real boyfriend for twenty-five days, during which time I had spoken to him exactly three times on the phone, was already in danger of losing him to someone with multicolored eyes, and said so.

"Well, I'm sorry, Amelia," Grandmère said. "But I can't say you know what you're about if it's true you actually want to keep this young man."

I swear I do not know what came over me at that moment. But it was like all the pressure that had been building up—the parking-meter thing; missing Michael and my mom and Fat Louie; what I was going to say to Prince William; my zit—all became too much, and I heard myself spewing, "Of course I want to keep him! But how am I going to be able to do that, when I am an entirely un–self-actualized, talentless, breastless, un–Kate-Bosworth-like princess FREAK?????"

Grandmère looked kind of surprised at my outburst. She didn't seem to know which issue to address first, my talentlessness or breastlessness. Finally she settled for saying, "Well, you could start by not staying on the phone with him until all hours of the night. You do not give him any reason to doubt your affections."

"Of course not," I said, horrified. "Why would I do that? I love him!"

"But you mustn't let him know that!" Grandmère looked ready to throw her mid-morning Sidecar at me. "Are you completely dense? *Never* let a man be sure of your affections for him! You did a very good job at first, with this business of forgetting his birthday. But now you are ruining everything with this calling all the time. If *that boy* realizes how you really feel, he will stop trying to please you."

"But Grandmère." I was way confused. "You married Grandpa. Surely he figured out you loved him if you went ahead and married him."

"Grandpère, Mia, please, not this vulgar *Grandpaw* you Americans insist upon." Grandmère sniffed and looked insulted. "Your grandfather most certainly did not 'figure out' my feelings for him. I made quite certain he thought I was only marrying him for his money and title. And I don't think I need to point out to you that we had forty blissful years together. And without separate bedrooms," she added, with some malice, "unlike *some* royal couples I could mention."

"Wait a minute." I stared at her. "For forty years, you slept in the same bed as Grandpère, but you never once told him that you loved him?"

Grandmère drained what was left of her Sidecar and laid an affectionate hand on top of Rommel's head. Since returning to Genovia and being diagnosed with OCD, most of Rommel's fur has started to grow back, thanks to the plastic cone around his head. White fuzz was starting to come out all over him, like down on a baby chicken. But it didn't make him look any less repulsive.

"That," Grandmère said, "is precisely what I am telling you. I kept your grandfather on his toes, and he loved every minute of it. If you want to keep this Michael fellow, I suggest you do the same thing. Stop this business of calling him every night. Stop this business of not looking at any other boys. And stop this obsessing over what you are going to get him for his birthday. *He* should be the one obsessing over what he is going to buy to keep *you* interested, not the other way around."

"*Me?* But my birthday isn't until May!" I didn't want to tell her that I had already figured out what I was getting for Michael. I didn't want to tell her because I had sort of snitched it out of the back of the Palais de Genovia museum.

Well, nobody else was using it, so I don't see why I can't. I'm the Princess of Genovia, after all. I own everything in that museum anyway. Or at least the royal family does.

"Who says a man should give a woman gifts only on her birthday?" Grandmère was looking at me like she pretty much despaired of me as a Homo sapien. She held up her wrist. Dripping from it was a bracelet Grandmère wears a lot, one with diamonds big as Euro one-cent pieces hanging off it. "I got this from your grandfather on March fifth, forty years or so ago. Why? March fifth is not my birthday, nor is it any kind of holiday. Your grandfather gave it to me on that day merely because he thought that the bracelet, like me, was exquisite." She lowered her hand back down to Rommel's head. "That, Amelia, is how a man ought to treat the woman he loves."

All I could think was, *Poor Grandpère.* He couldn't have had any idea what he was getting himself into when it came to Grandmère, who'd been a total babe back when she was young, before she'd gotten her tattooed eyeliner and shaved off her eyebrows. I'm sure Gramps just took one look at her across that dance floor where they met back when he was just the dashing heir to the throne and she was a pert young debutante, and froze, like a graffiti artist caught in a cop car's headlights, never suspecting what lay ahead. . . .

Years of subtle mind games and Sidecar shaking.

"I don't think I can be like that, Grandmère," I said. "I mean, I don't want Michael to give me diamonds. I just want him to ask me to the Prom."

"Well, he won't do it," Grandmère said, "if he doesn't think there's a possibility you're entertaining offers from other boys."

"Grandmère!" I was shocked. "I would never go to the Prom with anybody but Michael!" Not like there was a big chance of anybody else asking me, either, but I felt that was beside the point.

"But you must never let him *know* that, Amelia," Grandmère said, severely. "You must keep him always in doubt of your feelings, always on his toes. Men enjoy the hunt, you see, and once they have taken their quarry, they tend to lose all interest. Here. This is for you to read. I believe it will adequately illustrate my point."

Grandmère had drawn out a book from her Gucci bag and handed it to me. I looked down at it incredulously.

"*Jane Eyre*?" I couldn't believe it. "Grandmère, I

saw the movie. And no offense, but it was way boring."

"Movie," Grandmère said with a sniff. "Read that book, Amelia, and see if it doesn't teach you a thing or two about how men and women relate to one another."

"Grandmère," I said, not sure how to break it to her that she was way behind the times. "I think people who want to know how men and women relate to one another are reading *Men Are from Mars, Women Are from Venus* these days."

"READ IT!" Grandmère yelled, so loudly that she scared Rommel clear off her lap. He slunk off to cower behind a potted geranium.

I swear, I don't know what I did to deserve a grandmother like mine. Lilly's grandma totally worships Lilly's boyfriend, Boris Pelkowski. She is always sending him Tupperware tubs of kreplach and stuff. I don't know why I have to get a grandmother who is already trying to get me to break up with a guy I've only been going out with for twenty-five days.

Seven days, six hours, forty-two minutes until I see him again.

Tuesday, January 13
Royal Daily Schedule

8 a.m.–10 a.m.
Breakfast with members of Royal Genovian Shakespeare Society

Jane Eyre v. boring—so far nothing but orphanages, bad haircuts, and a lot of coughing.

10 a.m.–4 p.m.
Session of Genovian Parliament

Jane Eyre looking up—she has gotten a job as governess in house of very rich guy, Mr. Rochester. Mr. Rochester v. bossy, much like Wolverine, or Michael.

5 p.m.–7 p.m.
Tea with Grandmère and wife of prime minister of England

Mr. Rochester=hottie. Going on my list of Totally Hot Guys, between Hugh Jackman and that Croatian dude from *ER*.

8 p.m.–10 p.m.
Formal State dinner with prime minister of England and family

Jane Eyre=total idiot! It was not Mr. Rochester's

fault! Why is she being so mean to him?

And Grandmère shouldn't yell at me for reading at the table. She's the one who gave me this book in the first place.

Six days, eleven hours, twenty-nine minutes until I see him again.

Wednesday, January 14, 3 a.m., Royal Genovian bedchamber

Okay, I guess I understand what Grandmère was getting at with this book. But seriously, that whole part where Mrs. Fairfax warns Jane not to get too chummy with Mr. Rochester before the wedding was just because back in those days there was no birth control.

Still—and I may have to consult with Lilly on this—I am pretty sure it is unwise to pattern one's behavior after the advice of a fictional character, especially one from a book written in 1846.

However, I do get the general gist of Mrs. Fairfax's warning, which was this: Do not chase boys. Chasing boys is bad. Chasing boys can lead to horrible things like mansions going up in flames, hand amputations, and blindness. Have some self-respect and don't let things go too far before the wedding day.

I get this. I so get this.

But what is Michael going to think if I just stop calling???? I mean, he might think I don't like him anymore!!!! And it isn't like I've got so much going for me in the first place. I mean, as a girlfriend, I pretty much suck. I'm not good at anything, I can't remember people's birthdays, and I'm a *princess*.

I guess that is Grandmère's point. I guess you are supposed to keep boys on their toes this way.

I don't know. But it seemed to work with Grand-père. And for Jane, in the end. I guess I could give it a try.

But it won't be easy. It is nine o'clock at night in Florida right now. Who knows what Michael is doing? He might have gone down to the beach for a stroll and met some beautiful homeless musician girl, who is living on the boardwalk and making a living off the tourists, for whom she plays wryly observant folk songs on her Stratocaster. I can't even play *tennis*, let alone an instrument.

I bet she is wearing fringy things and is all busty and snaggle-toothed, like Jewel. No boy could be expected just to walk on by when a girl like that is standing there.

No. Grandmère and Mrs. Fairfax are right. I've got to resist. I've got to resist the urge to call him. When you are less available, it drives men wild, just like in *Jane Eyre*.

Though I think changing my name and running away to live with distant relations like Jane did might be going a bit too far. As appealing as it seems.

Five days, seven hours, and twenty-five minutes until I see him again.

Wednesday, January 14
Royal Daily Schedule

8 a.m.–10 a.m.
Breakfast with Genovian Society of Medicine
So, so tired. This is the last time I stay up half the night reading nineteenth-century literature.

10 a.m.–4 p.m.
Session of Genovian Parliament
Filibuster by minister of finance! He says Genovia will have parking meters or perish!

5 p.m.–7 p.m.
Session of Genovian Parliament
Filibuster ongoing. Would like to slip out for an Orangina, but am afraid this would look unsupportive.

8 p.m.–10 p.m.
Session of Genovian Parliament
Can't take it anymore. Filibuster too boring. Plus René just poked his head in and smirked at me. Let him laugh. *He* won't have to rule a country someday.

Thursday, January 15,
State dinner in neighboring Monaco

Grandmère finally noticed my zit. I guess the idea of me meeting Prince William with a giant zit on my chin was too much for her, since she completely flipped out. I told her I had the situation under control, but Grandmère clearly does not put as much faith in toothpaste as a complexion aid as I do. She sent for the Royal Dermatologist. He injected my chin with something, then said not to put any more toothpaste on my face.

I can't even seem to handle a zit right. How am I ever going to rule a country?

TO DO BEFORE LEAVING GENOVIA

1. Find a safe place to put Michael's present where it will NOT be found by grandmother or nosy ladies-in-waiting while packing my stuff (inside toe of combat boot?).

2. Say good-bye to kitchen staff, and thank them for all the vegetarian fare.

3. Make sure harbormaster has hung pair of scissors off every buoy in port for use of yachting

tourists who didn't bring along their own set to snip six-pack holders.

4. Take funny nose and glasses off the statue of Grandmère in the Portrait Hall before she notices.

5. Practice my "Meeting Prince William" speech. Also "Good-bye Prince René" speech.

6. Break François's record of twenty feet, seven inches sock-sliding along Crystal Hallway.

7. Let all the doves in the palace dovecote go (if they want to come back, that is fine, but they should have the option to be free).

8. Let Tante Jean Marie know that this is the twenty-first century and that women no longer have to live with the stigma of dark facial hair, and leave her my Jolen.

9. Slip minister of finance details on parking-meter manufacturers that I got off the Internet.

10. Get scepter back from Prince René.

Tina spent all day yesterday reading *Jane Eyre* per my recommendation and agrees with me that there might be something to the whole letting-boys-chase-you-as-opposed-to-you-chasing-them thing. So she has decided not to e-mail or call Dave (unless he e-mails or calls first, of course).

Lilly, however, refuses to take part in this scheme, as she says game playing is for children and that her relationship with Boris is one that cannot be qualified by modern-day psychosexual mating practices. According to Tina (I can't call Lilly because Michael might pick up the phone and then he'll think I'm chasing him), Lilly says that *Jane Eyre* was one of the first feminist manifestos, and she heartily approves of us using it as a model for our romantic relationships. Although she sent a warning to me through Tina that I shouldn't expect Michael to ask me to marry him until after he's gotten at least one postgraduate degree, as well as a starting position with a company that pays at least two hundred thousand dollars a year, plus annual performance bonus.

Lilly also added that the one time she saw him ride a horse, Michael looked way unromantic, so I shouldn't get my hopes up that he's going to be jumping any stiles, like Mr. Rochester, any time soon.

But I find this hard to believe. I am sure Michael would look very handsome on a horse.

Tina mentioned that Lilly is still upset about the movie of my life they showed the other day. Tina saw it, though, and said it wasn't as bad as Lilly is making it out to be. She said the lady who played Principal Gupta was hilarious.

But Tina wasn't in the movie, on account of her dad having found out about it beforehand and threatening the filmmakers with a lawsuit if they mentioned his daughter's name anywhere. Mr. Hakim Baba worries a lot about Tina getting kidnapped by a rival oil sheik. Tina says she wouldn't mind being kidnapped though if the rival oil sheik was cute and willing to commit to a long-term relationship and remembered to buy her one of those diamond heart pendants from Kay Jewelers on Valentine's Day.

Tina says the girl who played Lana Weinberger in the movie did a fabulous job and should get an Emmy. Also that she didn't think Lana was going to be too happy about how she was portrayed, as a jealous princess wannabe.

Also the guy who played Josh was a babe. Tina is trying to find his e-mail address.

Tina and I vowed that if either of us ever felt like calling our boyfriends, instead we would call each other. Unfortunately I have no cell phone so it is not like Tina will be able to reach me if I am in the middle of knighting someone or anything. But I am fully going to hit my dad up for a Motorola tomorrow. Hey, I am heir to the sovereign of an entire country. At the very least I should have a beeper.

Note to self: look up word "stile."

Four days, twelve hours, and five minutes until I see Michael again.

Saturday, January 17,
Royal Genovian Polo Match

Could there be a more boring sport than polo? I mean, besides golf? I think not.

Furthermore, I do not think it is very good for the horses, swinging mallets that close to their heads. It is like Silver, the Lone Ranger's horse. The Lone Ranger kept shooting off guns next to Silver's ear. It was no wonder the poor thing kept rearing.

Also, René isn't *too* competitive with Prince William, or anything. René keeps riding in front of the poor guy and stealing the ball from him every chance he gets . . . and they are supposed to be on the same team!

I swear, if René's team wins, and he pulls a Mia Hamm and swings his shirt around over his head, I will know he is just doing all of this for the benefit of the hordes of Prince William fans who are here. Which I guess is understandable. It probably is disconcerting to him that Wills is so much more popular than he is. And René does have pretty impressive pecs.

If only all those girls knew about the Enrique Iglesias lip-synching. . . .

Three days, seventeen hours, and six minutes until I see Michael again. Talk about impressive pecs . . .

Saturday, January 17, 11 p.m.,
Royal Genovian bedchamber

Grandmère so needs to get a life.

Tonight was the Farewell Ball—you know, to cele-
brate the end of my first official trip to Genovia in my
capacity as heir to the throne.

Anyway, Grandmère's been going on about this ball
for weeks, like this is going to be my big chance to
redeem myself for the whole parking-meter thing. Not
to mention the Prince William factor. In fact, between
that and the whole not-thinking-Michael-suitable-
consort-material, she's been laying it on so thick, I fully
blame her for my zit—even though it's gone now, thanks
to the miracle of modern dermatology. But still.
Between the pressures Grandmère has been putting on
me, plus the anxiety of knowing that my boyfriend
might at this very moment be taking surfing lessons
from some zit-free Kate Bosworth type, it is a wonder
my complexion does not resemble that guy's they kept
locked in the basement in that movie *The Goonies*.

Whatever. So Grandmère makes this big deal out
of my hair (growing out and so becoming triangular-
shaped again, but who cares, boys are supposed to like
girls with long hair better than girls with short hair—I
read that in French *Cosmo*) and she makes this big deal
out of my fingernails (okay, so in spite of the whole
New Year's resolution thing I still keep biting them. So

sue me. The man is keeping me down.) and she makes this big deal out of what I am going to say to Prince William.

Then, after all this, we get to the stupid ball, and I walk up to Wills (who I will admit—though my heart still belongs to Michael—was looking quite studly in his tux) and I'm all set to go, "It's very nice to meet you," but it was like at the last second I forgot who I was talking to, because he turned those blue, blue eyes on me, like a pair of klieg lights, and I totally froze up, exactly the way I did that time Josh Richter smiled at me in Bigelow's Drugstore. Seriously, like, I couldn't remember where I was or what I was doing there, I was just looking into those blue eyes and going, inside my head, *Oh, my God, they're the color of the sea outside the window of my Royal Genovian bedchamber.*

Then Prince William was going, "It's very nice to meet you," and shaking my hand, and I just kept on staring at him, even though I do not even like him in that way. I AM IN LOVE WITH MY BOYFRIEND.

But I guess that is the thing with the guy, he has that whole charisma thing going, kind of like Bill Clinton (only I never met him; I just read about it).

Anyway, that was it. That was the extent of my interaction with Prince William of England! He turned around after that to answer someone's question about Thoroughbred horse racing, and I was like, "Oh, look, baked mushroom caps," to cover my excruciating mortification and went chasing after the footman who was passing them around. That's all, the end.

Needless to say, I did not get his e-mail address. Tina is just going to have to learn to live with disappointment.

Oh, but my evening did not end there. Not at all. No, little did I know there was much, much more to come, in the form of Grandmère shoving me at *Prince René* all night, so that the two of us could dance in front of this *Newsweek* reporter who is in Genovia to do a story on our country's transition to the Euro. She SWORE that was the only reason: for the photo op.

But then while we were dancing—which, by the way, I am horrible at . . . dancing, I mean. I can box step if I look down the whole time and count inside my head, but that is about it, aside from slow dancing, but guess what? They so don't slow dance in Genovia . . . at least, not in the palace—I saw Grandmère totally going around, pointing us out to people, and it was so obvious what she was saying, you didn't even have to be a lip reader to know she was going, "Aren't they just the loveliest couple?"

EW!!!

So then when the dance was over, just in case Grandmère was getting any ideas, I went up to her and I was all, "Grandmère, I am willing to cool it with the calling-Michael stuff, but that does not mean I am going to start going out with Prince René," who, by the way, asked me if I wanted to step outside onto the terrazzo and have a smoke.

I of course told him I do not smoke and that he shouldn't either as tobacco is responsible for half a million deaths a year in the United States alone, but he only laughed at me, all James Spader from *Pretty in Pink*-ishly.

So then I told him not to get any big ideas, that I already have a boyfriend and that maybe he didn't see the movie of my life, but I fully know how to handle guys who are only after me for my crown jewels.

So then René said I was adorable and I said, "Oh, for God's sake, cut the Enrique Iglesias act," and then my dad came up and asked me if I had seen the prime minister of Greece and I said, "Dad, I think Grandmère is trying to fix me up with René," and then my dad got all tight-lipped and took Grandmère aside and had "A Word" with her while Prince René slunk off to go make out with one of the Hilton sisters.

Afterward Grandmère came up and told me not to be so ridiculous, that she merely wanted Prince René and I to dance together because it was a nice photo op for *Newsweek* and that maybe if they ran a story on us, it would attract more tourists.

To which I replied that in light of our crumbling infrastructure, more tourists is exactly what this country doesn't need.

I suppose if my palace had been bought out from under me by some shoe designer, I would be pretty desperate, too, but I wouldn't hit on a girl who has the weight of an entire populace on her shoulders—and already *has* a boyfriend, besides.

On the bright side, if *Newsweek* does run the photo, maybe Michael will get all jealous of René the way Mr. Rochester did of that St. John guy, and he'll boss me around some more!!!

Two days, eight hours, and ten minutes until I see Michael again.

I CAN'T WAIT!!!!!!!!!!!!!!

I cannot believe that

A. my dad is staying in Genovia in order to
   resolve the parking crisis rather than coming
   back to New York with me.

B. he actually believed Grandmère when she said
   due to my poor performance in Genovia that
   my princess lessons need to continue.

C. she (not to mention Rommel) is coming back to
   New York with me.

IT IS NOT FAIR. I held up my part of the agreement. I went to every single princess lesson Grandmère
gave last fall. I passed Algebra. I gave my stupid
address to the Genovian people.

Grandmère says that in spite of what I might think,
I still have a lot to learn about governance. Except that
she is so wrong. I know she is only coming back to New
York with me so she can go on torturing me. It is kind
of like her hobby now. In fact, for all I know, it might
even be her gift, her God-given talent.

At least she is lucky enough to have one. But it is
still so not fair.

And yes, before I left, my dad slipped me a hundred Euros and told me if I didn't make a fuss about Grandmère, he'd make it up to me someday.

But there is nothing he can do to make *this* up to me. Nothing.

He says she is just a harmless old lady and that I should try to enjoy her while I can because someday she won't be with us anymore. I just looked at him like he was crazy. Even he couldn't keep a straight face. He went, "Okay, I'll donate *two* hundred bucks a day to Greenpeace if you keep her out of my hair."

Which is funny, because of course my dad hasn't got any. Hair, I mean.

That is double the amount he was already donating in my name to my favorite organization. I sincerely hope Greenpeace appreciates the supreme sacrifice I am making for its sake.

So Grandmère is coming back to New York with me, and dragging a cowering Rommel along with her. Just when his fur had started to grow back, too. Poor thing.

I told my dad I'd put up with the whole princess-lesson thing again this semester, but that he'd better get one thing straight with Grandmère beforehand, and that is this: I have a serious boyfriend now. Grandmère had better not try to sabotage this, or think she can be trying to fix me up with any more Prince Renés. I don't care how many crown titles the guy has, my heart belongs to Mr. Michael Moscovitz, Esquire.

My dad said he'd see what he could do. But I don't know how much he was actually paying attention, since Miss Czech Republic was hanging around, twirling her sash kind of impatiently.

Anyway, a little while ago I told Grandmère myself that she better watch it where Michael is concerned.

"I don't want to hear anything more about how I'm too young to be in love," I said, over the lunch (poached salmon for Grandmère, three-bean salad for me) served by the royal Genovian flight attendants. "I am old enough to know my own heart, and that means I am old enough to give that heart away if I choose to."

Grandmère said something about how then I should get ready for some heartburn, but I ignored her. Just because her romantic life since Grandpa died has been less than satisfactory is no reason for her to be so cynical about mine. I mean, that is just what she gets for going out with media moguls and dictators and stuff.

Michael and I, on the other hand, are going to have a great love, just like Jane and Mr. Rochester. Or Jennifer Aniston and Brad Pitt.

Or at least we will, if we ever actually get to go out on a date.

One day, fourteen hours until I see him again.

Monday, January 19,
Martin Luther King Day, the loft, at last

I am so happy I feel like I could burst, just like that eggplant I once dropped out of Lilly's sixteenth-floor bedroom window.

I'm home!!!!!!! I'm finally home!!!!!!

I cannot tell you how good it felt to look out the window of the airplane and see the bright lights of Manhattan below me. It brought tears to my eyes, knowing I was once again in the air space over my beloved city. Below me, I knew, cab drivers were running down little old ladies (unfortunately not Grandmère), deli owners were shortchanging their customers, investment bankers were not cleaning up after their dogs, and people all over town were having their dreams of becoming singers, actors, musicians, novelists, or dancers completely crushed by soulless producers, directors, agents, editors, and choreographers.

Yes, I was back in my beautiful New York. I was back home at last.

I especially knew it when I stepped off the plane, and there was Lars waiting for me, ready to take over bodyguarding duty from François, the guy who had looked after me in Genovia and who had taught me all the French swear words. Lars looked especially menacing on account of being all darkly tanned from his month off. He had spent his winter break with Tina

Hakim Baba's bodyguard, Wahim, snorkeling and hunting wild boar in Belize. He gave me a piece of ivory tusk as a memento of his trip, even though of course I don't approve of killing animals recreationally, even wild boars, who really can't help being so ugly and mean.

Then, after a delay of sixty-five minutes, thanks to a pileup on the Belt Parkway, I was home.

It was so good to see my mom!!!!! Her belly is starting to show now. I didn't want to say anything, because even though my mom says she does not believe in the Western standard of idealized beauty and that there is nothing wrong with a woman who is bigger than a size eight, I'm pretty sure though that if I had said anything like, "Mom, you're huge," even in a complimentary fashion, she would start to cry. After all, she still has quite a few months left to go.

So instead I just went, "That baby has to be a boy. Or if it's not, it's a girl who is going to be as tall as me."

"Oh, I hope so," my mom said, as she brushed tears of joy from her face—or maybe she was crying because Fat Louie was biting her ankles so hard in his effort to get near me. "I could use another you for when you aren't around. I missed you so much! There was no one to berate me for ordering roast pork and wonton soup from Number One Noodle Son."

"I tried," Mr. Gianini assured me.

Mr. G looks great, too. He is growing a goatee. I pretended I liked it.

Then I bent down and picked up Fat Louie, who was yowling to get my attention, and gave him a great big hug. I may be wrong, but I think he lost weight while I was away. I do not want to accuse anyone of purposefully starving him, but I noticed his dry food bowl was not completely full. In fact, it was perilously close to being only half full. I always keep Fat Louie's bowl filled to the brim, because you never know when there might be a sudden plague, killing everyone in Manhattan but cats. Fat Louie can't pour out his own food, having no thumbs, so he needs a little extra just in case we all die and there is no one around to open the bag for him.

But the loft looks so great!!!!!!!! Mr. Gianini did a lot to it while I was gone. He got rid of the Christmas tree—the first time in the history of the Thermopolis household that the Christmas tree was out of the loft by Easter—and had the place wired for DSL. So now you can e-mail or go on the Internet anytime you want, without tying up the phone.

It is like a Christmas miracle.

And that's not all. Mr. G also fully redid the darkroom, leftover from when my mom was going through her Ansel Adams stage. He pulled the boards off the windows and got rid of all the noxious chemicals that have been sitting around since forever because my mom and I were too afraid to touch them. Now the darkroom is going to be the baby's room! It is so sunny and nice in there. Or at least it *was*, until my mom started painting the walls (in egg tempera, of course, so as not to jeopardize the welfare of her unborn child!) with scenes of important historical significance, such as the trial of Winona Ryder and the engagement of J.Lo and Ben Affleck, so that, she says, the baby will have an understanding of all the problems facing our nation (Mr. G assured me privately that he is going to have the whole thing painted over as soon as my mom gets admitted to the maternity ward. She will never know the difference once the endorphins kick in. All I can say is thank God Mom picked a man with so much common sense with whom to reproduce this time around).

But the best thing of all was what was waiting for me on the answering machine. My mom played it for me proudly almost the minute I walked through the door.

IT WAS A MESSAGE FROM MICHAEL!!!! MY FIRST RECORDED MESSAGE FROM MICHAEL SINCE I BECAME HIS GIRL-FRIEND!!!!!!!!!!!!

Which of course means it worked. The my-not-calling-him thing, I mean.

The message goes like this:

> *"Uh, hi, Mia? Yeah, it's Michael. I was just wondering if you could, uh, call me when you get this message. 'Cause I haven't heard from you in*

a while. And I just want to know if you're, uh,
okay. And make sure you got home all right. And
that there's nothing wrong. Okay. That's all.
Well. Bye. This is Michael, by the way. Or
maybe I said that. I can't remember. Hi, Mrs.
Thermopolis. Hi, Mr. G. Okay. Well.
Call me, Mia. Bye."

I took the tape out of the message machine and am
keeping it in the drawer of my nightstand along with

    A. some grains of rice from the bag Michael and I
       sat on at the Cultural Diversity Dance, in
       memory of the first time we ever slow danced
       together;

    B. a dried-out piece of toast from the *Rocky Horror*
       Show, which is where Michael and I went on
       our first date, though it wasn't really a date
       because Kenny came, too; and

    C. a cut-out snowflake from the Non-
       denominational Winter Dance, in memory of
       the first time Michael and I kissed.

It was the best Christmas present I could ever have
gotten, that message. Even better than DSL.

So then I came into my room and unpacked and

played the message over about fifty times on my tape player, and my mom kept coming in to give me more hugs and asking me if I wanted to listen to her new Liz Phair CD and wanting to show me her stretch marks. Then about the thirtieth time she came in, I was playing Michael's message again, and she was all, "Haven't you called him back yet, honey?" and I went, "No," and she went, "Well, why not?" and I went, "Because I am trying to be like Jane Eyre."

And then my mom got all squinty-eyed like she does whenever they are debating funding for the arts on C-SPAN.

"Jane Eyre?" she echoed. "You mean the book?"

"Exactly," I said, tugging the little Napoleonic diamond napkin holders that the prime minister of France had given me for Christmas out from beneath Fat Louie, who had laid down inside my suitcase, I guess in the mistaken belief that I was packing, not unpacking, and he wanted to try to stop me from going away again. "See, Jane didn't chase Mr. Rochester, she let him chase her. And so Tina and I, we've both taken solemn vows that we are going to be just like Jane."

Unlike Grandmère, my mom didn't look happy to hear this.

"But Jane Eyre was so mean to poor Mr. Rochester!" she cried.

I didn't mention that this was what I had thought, too . . . at first.

"Mom," I said, very firmly. "What about the whole keeping Bertha locked up in the attic thing?"

"Because she was a lunatic," my mom pointed out. "It wasn't like they had psychotropic drugs back then. Keeping Bertha locked in the attic was kinder, really, than sending her to a mental hospital, considering what they were like during that era, with people chained to the walls. Really, Mia. I swear I don't know where you get half your ideas. Jane Eyre? Who told you about Jane Eyre?"

"Um," I said, stalling because I knew my mom wasn't going to like the answer. "Grandmère."

My mom's lips got so thin, they completely disappeared.

"I should have known," she said. "Well, Mia, I think it is commendable that you and your friends have decided not to chase boys. However, if a boy leaves a nice message on the answering machine like Michael did, it could hardly be construed as chasing for you to do the polite thing and return his call."

I thought about this. My mom was probably right. I mean, it isn't as if Michael has a crazy wife in the attic. The Fifth Avenue apartment where the Moscovitzes live doesn't even have an attic, so far as I know.

"Okay," I said, setting down the clothes I'd been putting away. "I guess I could return his call." My heart was swelling at the very idea. In a minute—less than a minute, if I could get my mom out of my room fast enough—I'd be talking to Michael! And there wouldn't be that weird swooshing sound there always is when you call from across the ocean. Because there would be no ocean separating us! Just Washington Square Park. And I wouldn't have to worry about him wishing I were Kate Bosworth instead of Mia Thermopolis, because there are no Kate Bosworth types in Manhattan . . . or at least if there are, they have to keep their clothes on, at least in winter.

"Returning calls probably doesn't count as chasing," I said. "That would probably be okay."

My mom, who was sitting on the end of my bed, just shook her head.

"Really, Mia," she said. "You know I don't like to contradict your grandmother"—this was the biggest lie I'd heard since René told me I waltzed divinely, but I let it slide, on account of Mom's condition—"but I really don't think you should be playing mind games with boys. Particularly a boy you care about. Particularly a boy like Michael."

"Mom, if I want to spend the rest of my life with him, I have to play games with Michael," I explained to her, patiently. "I certainly can't tell him the truth. If he were ever to learn the depths of my passion for him, he'd run like a startled fawn."

My mom looked stunned. "A what?"

"A startled fawn," I explained. "See, Tina told her

boyfriend Dave Farouq El-Abar how she really feels about him, and he pulled a total David Caruso on her."

My mom blinked. "A who?"

"David Caruso," I said. I felt sorry for my mom. Clearly she had only managed to snag Mr. Gianini by the skin of her teeth. I couldn't believe she didn't know this stuff. "You know, he disappeared for a really long time. Dave only resurfaced when Tina managed to scrounge Wrestlemania tickets for the Garden. And ever since, Tina says things have been really awkward." Done unpacking, I shooed Fat Louie out of the suitcase, closed it, and put it on the floor. Then I sat next to my mom on the bed. "Mom," I said. "I do *not* want that to happen to me and Michael. I love Michael more than anything else in the entire world, except for you and Fat Louie."

I just said the you part to be polite. I think I love Michael more than I love my mom. It sounds terrible to say, but I can't help it, it is just how I feel.

But I will never love anyone or anything as much as I love Fat Louie.

"So don't you see?" I said to her. "What Michael and I have, I don't want to mess it up. He's my Romeo in black jeans." Even though of course I have never seen Michael in black jeans. But I am sure he has some. It is just that we have a dress code at our school, so usually when I see him he is in gray flannel pants, as that is part of our uniform. "And the fact of the matter is,

Michael could do way better than me, anyway. So I have to be especially careful."

My mom blinked at me sort of confusedly. "Better than you? What on earth are you talking about, Mia?"

"Well, you know," I said. "I mean, Mom, I am not exactly a catch. I'm not really pretty, or anything, and I think we both know how hard I had to work just to pass my first semester of freshman Algebra. And it isn't as if I am really good at anything."

"Mia!" My mom looked totally shocked. "What are you talking about? You're good at lots of things! Why, you know everything there is to know about the environment and Iceland and what's playing on the Lifetime Channel. . . ."

I tried to smile encouragingly at her, like I actually thought these things were talents. I didn't want to make my mom feel bad for not having passed any of her artistic gifts on to me. That is totally not her fault, just some faulty DNA strand somewhere.

"Yeah," I said. "But, see, Mom, those aren't actually talents. Michael is gorgeous and smart and he can play a bunch of instruments and write songs and is good at just about everything, and it's really only a matter of time until he gets snatched up by some totally pretty girl who can surf, or whatever—"

"I don't know why," my mom said, "you think that just because you had to work a little harder at Algebra than other people in your class that you are not good at anything, or that Michael is going to take up with a girl who can surf. But I do think that if you haven't seen a boy in a month, and he leaves a message for you, the decent thing to do is to call him back. If you don't, I think you can pretty much guarantee he is going to run. And not like a startled fawn, either."

I blinked at my mom. She had a point. I saw then that Grandmère's scheme—you know, of always keeping the man you love guessing as to whether or not you love him back—had some pitfalls. Such as, he could just decide you don't like him, and take off, and maybe fall in love with some other girl of whose affection he could be assured, such as Judith Gershner, president of the Computer Club and all-around prodigy, even though supposedly she is dating a boy from Trinity, but you never know, that could be a ruse to lull me into a false sense of security about Michael and let my guard down, thinking he is safe from Judith's fruit-fly–cloning clutches. . . .

"Mia," my mom said, looking at me all concerned. "Are you all right?"

I tried to smile, but I couldn't. How, I wondered, could Tina and I have overlooked this very serious flaw in our plan? Even now, Michael could be on the phone with Judith or some other equally intellectual girl, talking about quasars or photons or whatever it is smart people talk about. Worse, he could be on the phone with Kate Bosworth, talking about wave surface.

"Mom," I said, standing up. "You have to go. I have to call him."

I was glad the panic that was clutching my throat wasn't audible in my voice.

"Oh, Mia," my mom said, looking pleased. "I really think you should. Charlotte Brontë is, of course, a brilliant author, but you've got to remember, she wrote *Jane Eyre* back in the 1840s, and things were a little different then—"

"Mom," I said. Lilly and Michael's parents, the Drs. Moscovitz, have this totally hardfast rule about calling after eleven on schoolnights. It is verboten. And it was practically eleven. And my mom was still standing there, keeping me from having the privacy I would need if I were going to make this all-important call.

"Oh," she said, smiling. Even though she is pregnant, my mom still looks like a total babe, with all this long black hair that curls just right. Clearly I inherited my dad's hair, which I've actually never seen, since he's always been bald since I've known him.

DNA is so unfair.

Anyway, FINALLY she left—pregnant women move *so* slowly, I swear you would think evolution would have made them quicker so they could get away from predators or whatever, but I guess not—and I lunged for the phone, my heart pounding because at last, AT LAST, I was going to get to talk to Michael, and my mom had even said that it was all right, that my calling him wouldn't count as chasing since he'd called me first. . . .

And just as I was about to pick up the receiver, the phone rang. My heart actually did this flippy thing inside my chest, like it does every time I see Michael. It was Michael calling, I just knew it. I picked up after the second ring—even though I didn't want him dumping me for some more attentive girl, I didn't want him to think I was sitting by the phone waiting for him to call, either—and said, in my most sophisticated tone, "Hullo?"

Grandmère's cigarette-ravaged voice filled my ear. "Amelia?" she rasped. "Why do you sound like that? Are you coming down with something?"

"Grandmère." I couldn't believe it. It was ten fifty-nine! I had exactly one minute left to call Michael without running the risk of the wrath of his parents. "I can't talk now. I have to make another call."

"*Pfuit!*" Grandmère made her noise of disapproval. "And who would you be calling at this hour, as if I didn't know?"

"Grandmère." Ten fifty-nine and a half. "It's okay. He called me first. I am returning his call. It is the polite thing to do."

"It's too late for you to be calling *that boy*," Grandmère said.

Eleven o'clock. I had missed my opportunity. Thanks to Grandmère.

"You'll see him at school tomorrow, anyway," she went on. "Now, let me speak to your mother."

"My mother?" I was shocked by this. Grandmère never talks to my mom, if she can help it. They haven't gotten along since my mom refused to marry my dad after she got pregnant with me, on account of her not wanting her child to be subjected to the vicissitudes of a progenitive aristocracy.

"Yes, your mother," Grandmère said. "Surely you've heard of her."

So I went out and passed the phone to my mom who was sitting out in the living room with Mr. Gianini, watching *The Anna Nicole Show*. I didn't tell her who was on the phone, because if I had, my mom would have told me to tell Grandmère that she was in the shower, and then I would have had to talk to her some more.

"Hello?" my mom said, all brightly, thinking it was one of her friends calling to comment on the hijinks of Howard K. Stern and Bobby Trendy. I slunk out as fast as I could. There were several heavy objects lying around the couch that my mom could have hurled in my direction if I'd stayed within missile range.

Back in my room, I thought sadly about Michael. What was I going to say to him tomorrow, when Lars and I pulled up in the limo to pick him and Lilly up before school? That I'd gotten in too late to call? What if he noticed my nostrils flaring as I spoke? I don't know if he's figured out that they do that when I lie, but I think I'd sort of mentioned it to Lilly, since I have a complete inability to keep my mouth shut about stuff I really should just keep to myself, and supposing she told him?

Then, as I sat there dejectedly on my bed, pretty sleepy because in Genovia it was five in the morning and I was totally jet-lagged, I had a brilliant idea. I could see if Michael was logged on, and instant message him! I could do it even though my mom was on the phone with Grandmère, because we have DSL now!

So I scrambled over to my computer and did just that. And he was online!

Michael, I wrote. *Hi, it's me! I'm home! I wanted to call you, but it's after eleven, and I didn't want your mom and dad to get mad.*

Michael has changed his screen name since the demise of *Crackhead*. He's no longer CracKing. He's LinuxRulz, in protest of the stranglehold Microsoft has on the software industry.

LINUXRULZ: Welcome home! It's good to hear from you. I was worried you were dead or something.

So he had noticed I'd stopped calling! Which meant the plan that Tina and I had come up with was working perfectly. At least so far.

FTLOUIE: No, not dead. Just super busy. You know, fate of the aristocracy resting on my shoulders and all of that. So should

Lars and I pick you and Lilly up for school tomorrow?

LINUXRULZ: That'd be good. What are you doing Friday?

What am I doing Friday? Was he asking me OUT? Were Michael and I actually going to have a date? At last????

I tried to type casually so he wouldn't know that I was so excited, I had already freaked Fat Louie out by jumping up and down in my computer chair and almost rolling over his tail.

FTLOUIE: Nothing, so far as I know. Why?

LINUXRULZ: Want to go to dinner at the Screening Room? They're showing the first *Star Wars*.

OH, MY GOD!!!!!!!! HE *WAS* ASKING ME OUT!!!!!!!!! Dinner and a movie. At the same time, because at the Screening Room you sit at a table and eat dinner while the movie is going. And *Star Wars* is only my favorite movie of all time, after *Dirty Dancing*. Could there BE a girl luckier than me? No, I don't think so. Bite me, Britney.

My fingers were trembling as I typed

FTLOUIE: I think that would be OK. I'll have to check with my mom. Can I let you know tomorrow?

LINUXRULZ: OK. So see you tomorrow? Around 8:15?

FTLOUIE: Tomorrow, 8:15.

I wanted to add something like I missed you or I love you, but I don't know, it just felt too weird, and I couldn't do it. I mean, it's embarrassing, telling the person you love that you love them. It shouldn't be, but it is. Also, it didn't seem like something Jane Eyre would do. Unless, you know, she had just discovered the man she loved had gone blind in a heroic attempt to rescue his crazy firebug wife from an inferno she'd set herself.

Asking me out to dinner and a movie didn't really seem the same, somehow.

Then Michael wrote

LINUXRULZ: Kid, I've been from one side of this galaxy to the other—

which is one of my favorite lines from the first *Star Wars*. So then I wrote

FTLOUIE: I happen to like nice men.

—jumping ahead to *The Empire Strikes Back*, to which Michael replied

LINUXRULZ: I'm nice.

Which is better than saying I love you, because right after Han Solo says that, he totally kisses Princess Leia. OH, MY GOD!!! It really is like Michael is Han Solo and I'm Princess Leia, because Michael is good at fixing stuff like hyper drives, and, well, I'm a princess, and I'm very socially conscious like Leia, and everything.

Plus Michael's dog, Pavlov, sort of looks like Chewbacca. If Chewbacca were a sheltie.

I could not imagine a more perfect date if I tried. Mom will let me go, too, because the Screening Room isn't that far away, and it's *Michael*, after all. Even Mr. Gianini likes Michael, and he doesn't like many of the boys who go to Albert Einstein—he says they are mostly all walking bundles of testosterone.

I wonder if Princess Leia ever read *Jane Eyre*. But maybe *Jane Eyre* doesn't exist in her galaxy.

I will never get to sleep now, I am too worked up. *I am going to see him in eight hours and fifteen minutes.*

And on Friday, I am going to be sitting next to him in a darkened room. All alone. With no one else around. Except all the waitresses and the other people at the movie.

The Force is *so* with me.

Tuesday, January 20,
first day of school after winter break,
Homeroom

I barely made it out of bed this morning. In fact, the only reason I was able to drag myself out from beneath the covers—and Fat Louie, who laid on my chest purring like a weedwhacker all night long—was the prospect of seeing Michael for the first time in thirty-two days.

It is completely cruel to force a person of my tender years, when I should be getting at least nine hours of sleep a night, to travel back and forth between two such drastically different time zones, with not even a single day of rest in between. I am still completely jet-lagged, and I am sure it is going to stunt not only my physical growth, (not in the height department because I am tall enough, thank you, but in the mammary-gland division, glands being very sensitive to things like disrupted sleep cycles) but my intellectual growth as well.

And now that I am entering the second semester of my freshman year, my grades are actually going to start to matter. Not that I intend to go to college or anything. At least not right away. I, like Prince William, intend to take a year off between high school and college. But I hope to spend it developing some kind of gift or talent, or, if I can't find one, volunteering for Greenpeace, hopefully in one of those boats that goes out between Japanese and Russian whaling ships and the whales. I don't think Greenpeace takes volunteers who don't have at least a 3.0 grade-point average.

Anyway, it was murder getting up this morning, especially when, after I'd dragged out my school uniform, I realized my Queen Amidala panties weren't in my underwear drawer. I have to wear my Queen Amidala underwear on the first day of every semester, or I'll have bad luck for the rest of the year. I *always* have good luck when I wear my Queen Amidala panties. For instance, I was wearing them the night of the Nondenominational Winter Dance, when Michael finally told me he loved me.

Not that he was IN LOVE with me, of course. But that he loved me. Hopefully not like a friend.

I have to wear my Queen Amidala panties on the first day of second semester, just like I'll have to send them to the laundry-by-the-pound place and get them washed before Friday so I can wear them on my date with Michael. Because I'm going to need extra good luck that night, if I'm going to have to compete with the Kate Bosworths of the world for his attentions . . . and also since I plan on giving Michael his birthday present that night. His birthday present that I'm hoping he'll like so much, he'll totally fall in love with me, if he hasn't already.

So I had to go into my mom's room, the one she shares with Mr. Gianini, and wake her up (thank God

Mr. G was in the shower, I swear to God if I'd had to see them in bed together in the condition I was in at that time, I'd have gone completely Anne Heche) and be all, "Mom, where's my Queen Amidala underwear?"

My mom, who sleeps like a log even when she isn't pregnant, just went, "Shurnowog," which isn't even a word.

"Mom," I said. "I need my Queen Amidala underwear. Where are they?"

But all my mom said was, "Kapukin."

So then I got an idea. Not that I really thought there was any way my mom wasn't going to let me go out with Michael, after her uplifting speech about him the night before. But just to make sure she couldn't back out of it, I went, "Mom, can I go with Michael for dinner and a movie at the Screening Room this Friday night?"

And she went, rolling over, "Yeah, yeah, scuniper."

So I got that taken care of.

But I still had to go to school in my regular underwear, which creeped me out a little, because there's nothing special about it, it is just boring and white.

But then I kind of perked up when I got in the limo, because of the prospect of seeing Michael and all.

But then I was like, Oh, my God, what was going to happen when I saw Michael? Because when you haven't seen your boyfriend in thirty-two days, you can't just be all, "Oh, hi," when you see him. You have to, like, give him a hug or *something*.

But how was I going to give him a hug in the car? With everyone watching? I mean, at least I wasn't going to have to worry about my stepdad, since Mr. G fully refuses to take the limo to school with me and Lars and Lilly and Michael every morning, even though we are all going to the same place. But Mr. Gianini says he likes the subway. He says it is the only time he gets to listen to music he likes (Mom and I won't let him play Blood, Sweat and Tears in the loft, so he has to listen to it on his Discman).

But what about Lilly? I mean, Lilly was totally going to be there. How can I hug Michael in front of Lilly? And okay, it is partly because of Lilly that Michael and I got together in the first place. But that does not mean that I feel perfectly comfortable participating in, you know, public displays of affection with him *right in front of her*.

If this were Genovia it would be all right to kiss him on both cheeks, because that is the standard form of greeting there.

But this is America, where you barely even shake hands with people, unless you're, like, the mayor.

Plus there was the whole Jane-Eyre thing. I mean, Tina and I had resolved we were not going to chase our boyfriends, but we hadn't said anything about how to greet them again after not having seen them for thirty-two days.

I was almost going to ask Lars what he thought I ought to do when I had a brainstorm right as we were pulling up to the Moscovitzes' building. Hans, the driver, was going to hop out and open the door for Lilly and Michael, but I went, "I've got it," and then *I* hopped out, instead.

And there was Michael, standing there in the slush, looking all tall and handsome and manly, the wind tugging at his dark hair. Just the sight of him set my heart going about a thousand beats per minute. I felt like I was going to melt. . . .

Especially when he smiled once he saw me, a smile that went all the way up to his eyes, which were as deeply brown as I remembered, and filled with the same intelligence and good humor that had been there the last time I had gazed into them, thirty-two days earlier.

What I could not tell was whether or not they were filled with love. Tina had said I'd be able to tell, just by looking into his eyes, whether or not Michael loved me. But the truth was, all I could tell by looking into his eyes was that Michael didn't find me utterly repulsive. If he had, he'd have looked away, the way I do when I see that boy in the caf at school who always picks the corn out of his chili.

"Hi," I said, my voice suddenly super-squeaky.

"Hi," Michael said, his voice not squeaky at all, but really very thrillingly deep and Wolverine-like.

So then we stood there with our gazes locked on each other, and our breath coming out in little puffs of white steam, and people hurrying down Fifth Avenue on the sidewalk around us, people I barely saw. I hardly even noticed Lilly go, "Oh, for Pete's sake," and stomp past me to climb into the limo.

Then Michael went, "It's really good to see you."

And I went, "It's really good to see you, too."

From inside the limo, Lilly went, "Hello, it's like two below outside, will you two hurry it up and get in here already?"

So then I went, "I guess we better—"

And Michael went, "Yeah," and put his hand on the limo door to hold it open for me. But as I started to duck in there, he put his other hand on my arm, and when I turned around to see what he wanted (even though I kinda already knew) he went, "So can you go, on Friday night?"

And I went, "Uh-huh."

And then he kind of pulled on my arm in a very Mr. Rochester-like manner, causing me to take a step closer, and faster than I'd ever seen him move before, he bent down and kissed me, right on the mouth, in front of his doorman and all the rest of Fifth Avenue!

I have to admit, Michael's doorman and all of the people passing by, including everyone on the M1 bus that went barreling down the street at that very moment, didn't seem to take very much notice that the Princess of Genovia was getting kissed right there in front of them.

But *I* noticed. *I* noticed, and it felt great. It made me feel like maybe all my worrying about whether Michael loved me as a potential life partner as opposed to just as a friend had maybe been stupid.

Because you don't kiss a friend like that.

I don't think.

So then I slid into the back of the limo with Lilly, a big silly smile on my face that I was totally afraid she might make fun of, but I couldn't help it, I was so happy, because in spite of not having on my Queen Amidala underwear, I was already having a good semester, and it wasn't even fifteen minutes old!

Then Michael got in beside me and closed the door, and Hans started to drive and Lars said, "Good morning," to Lilly and Michael and they said good morning back and I didn't even notice that Lars was smirking behind his latte until Lilly told me when we got out of the limo at school.

"Like," she said, "we didn't all know what you were doing out there."

But she said it in a nice way.

I was so happy, I hardly even heard what Lilly was talking about on our way in to school, which was the whole movie thing. She had sent, she said, a certified letter to the producers of the movie of my life, and had no response, even though they had had it for more than a week.

"It is," Lilly said, "just another example of how those Hollywood types think they can get away with whatever they want. Well, I'm here to tell them they can't. If I don't hear back from them by tomorrow, I'm going to the news media."

That got my attention. I blinked at her. "You mean you're going to have a press conference?"

"Why not?" Lilly shrugged. "You did it, and up until recently, you could barely formulate a coherent sentence in front of a camera. So how hard can it be?"

Wow. Lilly is really mad about this movie thing. I guess I'm going to have to watch it myself to see how bad it is. The other kids at school don't seem to have thought much about it. But then they were all in St. Moritz or their winter homes in Ojai when it came on. They were too busy skiing or having fun in the sun to watch any stupid made-for-TV movie about the life of one of their classmates.

From the looks of the number of casts people are wearing—Tina was by far not the only one to sprain something on her vacation—everyone had a much better time on their break than I did. Even Michael says he spent most of the time at his grandparents' condo sitting on the balcony and writing songs for his new band.

I guess I am the only one who passed the whole of my break sitting in parliamentary sessions, trying to negotiate parking rates for casino garages in downtown Genovia.

Still, it's good to be back. It's good to be back because for the first time in my whole entire academic career, the guy I like actually likes—maybe even loves—me back. And I get to see him between classes and in Gifted and Talented fifth period—

Oh, my God! I totally forgot! It's a new semester! They are assigning us all new schedules! They are passing them out at the end of Homeroom, after the announcements. What if Michael and I aren't in the same Gifted and Talented class anymore? I am not even supposed to be in Gifted and Talented at all, seeing as how I am neither. They only put me in there when it became clear I was flunking Algebra, so I have an extra period for independent study. I was supposed to be in Tech Ed for that period. TECH ED! WHERE THEY MAKE YOU BUILD SPICE RACKS!

Second semester is Domestic Arts. IF I GET PUT IN DOMESTIC ARTS THIS SEMESTER INSTEAD OF GIFTED AND TALENTED I WILL DIE!!!!!!!

Because I ended up getting a B minus in Algebra last semester. They don't give you independent study periods if you are making B minuses. B minus is considered good. Except, you know, to people like Judith Gershner.

Oh, God, I knew it. I just KNEW something bad was going to happen if I didn't wear my Queen Amidala underwear.

So if I'm not in G and T, then the only time I will see Michael will be at lunch and between classes. Because he is a senior, and I am only a freshman, so it's not like I'll be in advanced calculus with him, or that he'll be in French II with me.

And I might not even be able to see him at lunch! We could conceivably not have the same lunch periods!

And even if we do, what is the likelihood that Michael and I are even going to sit together at lunch? Traditionally I always have sat with Lilly and Tina, and Michael always has sat with the Computer Club and upperclassmen. Is he going to come sit by me now? No way can I go sit at *his* table. All those guys over there ever do is talk about things I don't understand, like how Steve Jobs sucks and how easy it is to hack into India's missile defense system. . . .

Oh, God, they are passing out the new class schedules now. Please don't let me be in Domestic Arts. PLEASE

PLEASE PLEASE PLEASE PLEASE PLEASE
PLEASE PLEASE PLEASE PLEASE PLEASE
PLEASE PLEASE PLEASE PLEASE PLEASE
PLEASE PLEASE PLEASE PLEASE PLEASE
PLEASE PLEASE PLEASE PLEASE PLEASE
PLEASE PLEASE PLEASE PLEASE PLEASE
PLEASE PLEASE PLEASE PLEASE PLEASE
PLEASE PLEASE PLEASE PLEASE PLEASE
PLEASE PLEASE PLEASE PLEASE PLEASE
PLEASE PLEASE PLEASE PLEASE PLEASE
PLEASE PLEASE PLEASE PLEASE PLEASE
PLEASE PLEASE PLEASE PLEASE PLEASE
PLEASE PLEASE PLEASE PLEASE PLEASE
PLEASE PLEASE PLEASE PLEASE PLEASE
PLEASE PLEASE PLEASE PLEASE PLEASE
PLEASE PLEASE PLEASE PLEASE PLEASE
PLEASE PLEASE PLEASE PLEASE PLEASE
PLEASE PLEASE PLEASE PLEASE PLEASE
PLEASE PLEASE PLEASE PLEASE PLEASE
PLEASE PLEASE PLEASE PLEASE PLEASE
PLEASE PLEASE PLEASE PLEASE PLEASE
PLEASE PLEASE PLEASE PLEASE PLEASE
PLEASE PLEASE PLEASE PLEASE PLEASE
PLEASE PLEASE PLEASE PLEASE PLEASE
PLEASE PLEASE PLEASE PLEASE PLEASE
PLEASE PLEASE PLEASE PLEASE PLEASE
PLEASE PLEASE PLEASE PLEASE PLEASE

Tuesday, January 20, Algebra

HA! My Queen Amidala underwear might be missing, but the power of the Force is with me nonetheless. My class schedule is EXACTLY the same as last semester's, except that by some miracle, I now have Bio third period instead of World Civ (Oh, God, please don't let Kenny, my former Bio partner and ex-boyfriend, have been switched to third-period Bio, too). World Civ is now seventh. And instead of PE fourth period, we all have Health and Safety.

And no Tech Ed or Domestic Arts, thank GOD!!!!! I don't know who told the administration that I am gifted and talented, but whoever it was, I am eternally grateful, and I will definitely try to live up to it.

And I happen to know that not only does Michael still have fifth-period G and T, but he has the same lunch hour as I do, too. I know that because after I got here to Algebra and sat down and got out my notebook and my Algebra I–II textbook, Michael came in!

Yes, he came right into Mr. G's second-semester freshman Algebra class, like he belonged there, or something, and everyone was staring at him, including Lana Weinberger, because you know seniors don't generally just go walking into freshman classes, unless they are working for the attendance office and bringing someone a hall pass or something.

But Michael doesn't work for the attendance office.

He popped into Mr. G's class just to see *me*. I know, because he came right up to my desk with his class schedule in his hand and went, "What lunch have you got?" and I told him, "A," and he said, "Same as me. You have G and T after?" and I said, "Yes," and he said, "Cool, see you at lunch."

Then he turned around and walked out again, looking all tall and collegiate with his JanSport backpack and New Balances.

And the way he said, "Hey, Mr. G," all casually to Mr. Gianini—who was sitting at his desk with a cup of coffee in his hands and his eyebrows all raised—as he went walking out . . .

Well, you just can't get cooler than that.

And he had been in here to see me. ME. MIA THERMOPOLIS. Formerly the most unpopular person in the entire school, with the exception of that guy who doesn't like corn in his chili.

So now everyone who had not seen Michael and me kissing at the Nondenominational Winter Dance knows that we are going out, because you don't walk into someone else's classroom between periods to look at their schedule unless you are dating.

I could feel all the gazes of my fellow Algebra sufferers boring into me, even as the bell was ringing, including Lana Weinberger's. You could practically hear everybody going, "*He*'s going out with *her*?"

I guess it *is* a little hard to believe. I mean, even *I*

can hardly believe it's true. Because of course it's common knowledge that Michael's the third best looking boy in the whole school, after Josh Richter and Justin Baxendale (though if you ask me, having seen Michael plenty of times without a shirt on, he makes those other guys look like that Quasimodo dude), so what is he doing with *me*, a talentless freak with feet the size of skis and no breasts to speak of and nostrils that flare when I lie?

Plus I am a lowly freshman, and Michael is a senior who has already been accepted early decision to an Ivy League school right here in Manhattan. Plus Michael is co-valedictorian of his class, being a straight-A student, whereas I barely scraped by Algebra I. Plus Michael is way involved with extracurriculars, including the Computer Club, Chess Club, and Physics Club. He designed the school's website. He can play, like, ten instruments. And now he is starting his own band.

Me? I'm a princess. That's about it.

And that's only *recently*. Before I found out I was a princess, I was just this massive reject who was flunking Algebra and always had orange cat hair all over her school uniform.

So yeah, I guess you could say that a lot of people were kind of surprised to see Michael Moscovitz come striding up to my desk in Algebra to compare class schedules. I could feel them all staring at me after he left and the bell rang, and I could hear them buzzing about it among themselves. Mr. G tried to bring everybody to order, going, "Okay, okay, break's over. I know it's been a long time since you last saw one another, but we've got a lot to tackle in the next nine weeks," only of course nobody paid any attention to him but me.

In the desk in front of me, Lana Weinberger was already on her cell phone—the new one that I'd paid for, on account of my having stomped her old one to bits in a semi-psychotic fit last month—going, "Shel? You are not going to *believe* what just happened. You know that freaky girl in your Latin class, the one with the TV show and the flat face? Yeah, well, her brother was just in here comparing class schedules with Mia Themopo—"

Unfortunately for Lana, Mr. Gianini has a thing about cell phone usage during class time. He fully pounced on her, snatched her phone away, put it up to his ear and said, "Ms. Weinberger can't speak to you right now as she is busy writing a thousand word essay on how rude it is to make cell phone calls during class time," after which he threw her phone in his desk drawer and told her she'd get it back at the end of the day, once she'd handed in her essay.

I wish Mr. G would give Lana's cell phone to me, instead. I would fully use it in a more responsible manner than she does.

But I guess even if the teacher is your stepdad, he

can't just confiscate things from other students and give them to you.

Which is a bummer because I could really use a cell phone right now. I just remembered I never asked my mom what Grandmère wanted when she called last night.

Oh, crud. Integers. Gotta go.

B = (x : x is an integer such that x > 0)

Defn: When integer is squared, the result is called a perfect square

Tuesday, January 20, Health and Safety

This is so boring —MT

You're telling me. How many times in our academic careers are they going to tell us having unprotected sex can result in unwanted pregnancy and AIDS? Do they think it didn't soak in the first five thousand times or something? —LM

Apparently. Hey, did you see Mr. Wheeton open the door to the teachers' lounge, look at Mademoiselle Klein, then leave? He is so obviously in love with her.

I know, you can totally tell, he is always bringing her lattes from Ho's. What is THAT about, if not luv? Wahim will be devastated if they start going out.

Yeah, but why would she choose Mr. Wheeton over Wahim? Wahim has all those muscles. Not to mention a gun.

Who can explain the vagaries of the human heart. Not I. Oh, my God, look, he's moving on to vehicular safety. Could this BE more boring? Let's make a list. You start it.

OK.

MIA THERMOPOLIS'S
NEW AND IMPROVED
LIST OF HOTTEST GUYS
with commentary by Lilly Moscovitz

1. Michael Moscovitz (*Obviously I can't agree due to genetic link to said individual. Will concede he is not hideously deformed.*)

2. Ioan Griffud from the *Horatio Hornblower* series (*Agreed. He can shiver me timbers anytime he wants.*)

3. The guy from *Smallville* (*Duh—only they should have him join the school swim team because he needs to take his shirt off more per episode.*)

4. Hayden Christensen (*Again, duh. Ditto swim team. There must be one for Jedis. Even ones who have embraced the Dark Side.*)

5. Mr. Rochester (*Fictional character, but I agree he exudes certain rugged manliness.*)

6. Patrick Swayze (*Um, okay, maybe in Dirty Dancing, but have you seen him lately? The guy is older than your dad!*)

7. Captain von Trapp from *The Sound of Music* (*Christopher Plummer was a hottie extraordinaire. I would pit him against the Nazi horde anytime.*)

8. Justin Baxendale (*Agree. I heard an eleventh grader tried to kill herself because he looked at her. Seriously. Like, his eyes were so hypnotic, she went full-on Sylvia Plath. She is in counseling now.*)

9. Heath Ledger (*Oooh, in the rock-and-roll knight movie, totally. Not so much in* Four Feathers, *though. I found his performance in that film somewhat stilted. Plus he didn't take his shirt off enough.*)

10. Beast from *Beauty and the Beast* (*I think I know someone else who needs counseling.*)

Tuesday, January 20, Gifted and Talented

I am so depressed.

I know I shouldn't be. I mean, everything in my life is going so great.

Great Thing Number One: The boy I have been madly in love with my entire life, practically, loves, or at least really likes, me back, and we are going out on our first real date on Friday.

Great Thing Number Two: I know it is only the first day of the new semester, but as of yet, I am not flunking anything, including Algebra.

Great Thing Number Three: I am no longer in Genovia, the most boring place on the entire planet, with the possible exception of Algebra class, and Grandmère's princess lessons.

Great Thing Number Four: I don't have Kenny for my Bio partner anymore. My new partner is Shameeka. What a relief. Which I know is cowardly (feeling relieved that I don't have to sit by Kenny anymore), but I am pretty sure Kenny thinks I am this horrible person to have led him on like that all those months, when really I liked someone else (though not the person he thought I liked). Anyway, the fact that I don't have to deal with any hostile looks from Kenny's direction (even though he fully has a new girlfriend, a girl from our Bio class, as a matter of fact—*he* didn't waste any time) is probably really going to boost my grade in that class. Plus Shameeka is really good at science. Actually Shameeka is really good at a lot of things, on account of her being a Pisces. But like me, Shameeka has no *one particular talent*, which makes her my soul sister, if you think about it.

Great Thing Number Five: I have really cool friends who seem actually to want to hang around with me, and not just because I am a princess, either.

But that, see, is the problem. I have all these great things going for me, and I should be totally happy. I should be over the moon with joy.

And maybe it's only the jet lag talking—I am so tired I can barely keep my eyes open—or possibly PMS—I am sure my internal clock is way messed up from all this transcontinental flying—but I can't shake this feeling that I am . . .

Well, a total reject.

I started to realize it today at lunch. I was sitting there like always with Lilly and Boris and Tina and Shameeka and Ling Su, and then Michael came and sat down with us, which of course caused this total cafeteria sensation, since usually he sits with the Computer

Club, and everyone in the entire school knows it.

And I was totally embarrassed but of course proud and pleased, too, because Michael *never* sat at our table back when he and I were just friends, so his sitting there *must* mean that he is at least slightly in love with me, because it is quite a sacrifice to give up the intellectual talk at the table where he normally sits for the kinds of talks we have at my table, which are generally, like, in-depth analyses of last night's episode of *Charmed* and how cute Rose McGowan's halter top was, or whatever.

But Michael was totally a good sport about it, even though he thinks *Charmed* is facile. And I really did try to steer the conversation around to things a guy would like, such as *Buffy the Vampire Slayer* or Milla Jovovich.

Only it turned out I didn't even need to, because Michael is like one of those lichen moths we read about in Bio. You know, the ones that turned black when the moss they fed on got all sooty during the industrial revolution? He can totally adapt to any situation, and feel at ease. This is an amazing talent that I wish I had. Maybe if I did, I wouldn't feel so out of place at meetings of the Genovian Olive Growers Association.

Anyway, today at the lunch table, someone brought up cloning, and everyone was talking about who would you clone if you could clone anyone, and people were saying, like, Albert Einstein so he could come back and tell us the meaning of life and stuff, or Jonas Salk so he could find a cure for cancer, and Mozart so he could finish his last requiem (whatever, that one was Boris's, of course), or Madame Pompadour so she could give us all tips on romance (Tina) or Jane Austen so she could write scathingly about the current political climate and we could all benefit from her cutting wit (Lilly).

And then Michael said he would clone Kurt Cobain, because he was a musical genius who died too young. And then he asked me who *I* would clone, and I couldn't think of anyone, because there really isn't anyone dead that I would want to bring back, except maybe Grandpère, but how creepy would that be? And Grandmère would probably freak. So I just said Fat Louie, because I love Fat Louie and wouldn't mind having two of him around.

Only nobody looked very impressed by this except for Michael who said, "That's nice," which he probably only said because he is my boyfriend.

But whatever, I could deal with that. I am totally used to being the only person I know who sits through *Empire Records* every time it comes on TBS and who thinks it is one of the best movies ever made—after *Star Wars* and *Dirty Dancing* and *Say Anything* and *Pretty Woman*, of course. Oh, and *Tremors* and *Twister*.

I am content to keep the fact that I must watch the Miss America Pageant every single year without fail secret, even though I know it is degrading to women and *not* a scholarship fund, considering no one bigger than a size ten ever gets into it.

I mean, I know these things about myself. It is just the way I am, and though I have tried to improve myself by watching award-winning movies such as *Crouching Tiger, Hidden Dragon* and *Gladiator*, I don't know, I just don't like them. Everybody dies at the end and besides if there is not dancing or explosions, it is very hard for me to pay attention.

So okay, I am trying to accept these things about myself. They are just the way I am. Like, I am good at English class and not so good at Algebra. Whatever.

But it wasn't until we got to Gifted and Talented today, after lunch, and Lilly started working on the shot list for this week's episode of her cable access show, *Lilly Tells It Like It Is*, and Boris got out his violin and started playing a concerto (sadly, not in the supply closet because they still haven't put the door back on it), and Michael put on headphones and started working on a new song for his band, that it finally hit me:

There is not one thing that I am particularly good at. In fact, if it weren't for the fact that I am a princess, I would be the most ordinary person alive. It is not even that I can't surf, or weave a friendship bracelet. I can't do *anything*.

I mean, all my friends have these incredible things they can do: Lilly knows everything there is to know and isn't shy about saying it in front of a camera. Michael can not only play guitar and, like, fifty other instruments including the piano and drums, but he can also design whole computer programs. Boris has been playing his violin at sold-out Carnegie Hall concerts since he was, like, eleven years old, or something. Tina Hakim Baba can read, like, a book a day, and retain what she's read and quote it back practically verbatim, and Ling Su is an extremely talented artist. The only person at our lunch table besides me who has no discernible special gift is Shameeka, and that made me feel better for about a minute, before I remembered that Shameeka is totally smart and beautiful and gets straight As and people who work at modeling agencies are always coming up to her in, like, Bloomingdale's when she is shopping with her mom and asking her to let them represent her (even though Shameeka's dad says over his dead body will any daughter of his be a model).

But me? I do not know why Michael even likes me, I am so talentless and boring. I mean, I guess it's a good thing my destiny as the monarch of a nation is sealed, because if I had to go apply for a job somewhere, I so fully wouldn't get it, because I'm not good at anything.

So here I am, sitting in Gifted and Talented, and there really is no getting around this basic fact:

I, Mia Thermopolis, am neither gifted nor talented.

WHAT AM I DOING IN HERE????? I DO NOT BELONG HERE!!!! I BELONG IN TECH ED!!!! OR DOMESTIC ARTS!!!!! I SHOULD BE MAKING A BIRDHOUSE OR A PIE!!!!

Just as I was writing this, Lilly leaned over and went, "Oh, my God, what is *wrong* with you? You look like you just ate a sock," which is what we say whenever someone looks super depressed, because that is how Fat Louie always looks whenever he accidentally eats one of my socks and has to go to the vet to have it surgically removed.

Fortunately Michael didn't hear her on account of having his headphones on. I would never have been able to confess in front of him what I confessed then to his sister, which is that I am a big talentless phony because then he would know I am nothing like Kate Bosworth and dump me.

"And they only put me in this class in the first place because I was flunking Algebra," I told her.

Then Lilly said the most surprising thing. Without batting an eye, she went, "You have a talent."

I stared at her, my own eyes wide and, I am afraid, filled with tears. "Oh, yeah, what?" I was really scared I was going to cry. It really must be PMS or something, because I was practically getting ready to start bawling.

But to my disappointment, all Lilly said was, "Well, if you can't figure it out, I'm not going to tell you." When I protested this, she went: "Part of the journey of achieving self-actualization is that you have to reach it on your own, without help or guidance from others. Otherwise, you won't feel as keen a sense of accomplishment. But it's staring you in the face."

I looked around, but I couldn't figure out what she was talking about. There was nothing staring me in the face that I could see. No one was looking at me at all. Boris was busy scraping away with his bow, and Michael was fingering his keyboard furiously (and silently), but that was about it. Everyone else was bent over their Kaplan review books or doodling or making sculptures out of Vaseline or whatever.

I still have no idea what Lilly is talking about. There is nothing I am talented at—except maybe telling a fish fork apart from a dinner one.

I can't believe that all I thought I needed in order to achieve self-actualization was the love of the man to whom I have pledged my heart. Knowing Michael loves me—or at least really likes me—just makes it all worse. Because his incredible talentedness makes the fact that I am not good at anything even more obvious.

I wish I could go to the nurse's office and take a nap. But they won't let you do that unless you have a temperature, and I'm pretty sure all I have is jet lag.

I knew it was going to be a bad day. If I had had on my Queen Amidala underwear, I never would have come face-to-face with the truth about myself.

Inventor	Invention	Benefits to Society	Cost to Society
Samuel F.B. Morse	Telegraph	Easier communication	Disrupted view (wires)
Thos. A. Edison	Electric light	Easier to turn on lights; Less expensive than candles	Society didn't trust them; weren't successful at first
Ben Franklin	Lightning rod	Less chance of house being struck	Ugly
Eli Whitney	Cotton gin	Less work	Less employment
A. Graham Bell	Telephone	Easier communication	Disrupted view (wires)
Elias Howe	Sewing machine	Less work	Less employment
Chris. Sholes	Typewriter	Easier work	Less employment
Henry Ford	Automobile	Faster Transportation	Pollution

I will never invent anything, either of benefit or cost to any society, because I am a talentless reject. I couldn't even get the country I will oneday rule to install PARKING METERS!!!!!!!!!!!!!

HOMEWORK

Algebra: probs at beginning of Chapter 11 (no review session, Mr. G has mtgs—also, just started semester, so nothing to review yet. Also, not flunking anymore!!!!!!)

English: update journal (How I Spent My Winter Break—500 words)

Bio: read Chapter 13

Health and Safety: read Chapter 1, You and Your Environment

G & T: figure out secret talent

French: Chapitre Dix

World Civ: Chapter 13: Brave New World

Tuesday, January 20, in the limo on way to Grandmère's for princess lesson

THINGS TO DO

1. Find Queen Amidala underwear.
2. Stop obsessing over whether or not Michael loves you vs. being in love with you. Be happy with what you have. Remember, lots of girls have no boyfriend at all. Or they have really gross ones with no front teeth like on Maury Povich.
3. Call Tina to compare notes on how not-chasing-boys thing is working.
4. Do all homework. Do not get behind first day!!!!!
5. Wrap Michael's present.
6. Find out what Grandmère talked to Mom about last night. Oh, God, please do not let it be something weird like wanting to take me skeet shooting. I don't want to shoot any skeets.
   Or anything else, for that matter.
7. Stop biting fingernails.
8. Buy cat litter.
9. Figure out secret talent. If Lilly knows, must be pretty obvious, as she hasn't even figured out about nostrils yet.

10. GET SOME SLEEP!!!!!!!!! Boys don't like
    girls who have huge, un–Kate-Bosworth-like
    purple bags under their eyes. Not even
    perfect boys like Michael.

Tuesday, January 20, still in the limo on way to Grandmère's for princess lesson

Draft for English Journal:

HOW I SPENT MY WINTER BREAK

I spent my winter break in Genovia, population 50,000. Genovia is a principality located on the Côte d'Azur between Italy and France. Genovia's main export is olive oil. Its main import is tourists. Recently, however, Genovia has begun suffering from considerable damage to its infrastructure due to foot traffic from the many cruise ships that dock in its harbor and

-

-

-

-

-

Wednesday, January 21, Homeroom

Oh, my God. I must have been even more tired than I thought yesterday. Apparently I fell asleep in the limo on the way to Grandmère's, and Lars couldn't even wake me up for my princess lesson! He says that when he tried, I swatted him away and called him a bad word in French (that is François's fault, not mine).

So he had Hans turn around and drive me back to the loft, then Lars carried me up three flights of stairs to my room (no mean feat, I weigh as much as about five Fat Louies), and my mom put me to bed.

I didn't wake up for dinner or anything. I slept until seven this morning! That is fifteen hours straight.

Wow. I must have been fried from all the excitement of being back home and seeing Michael, or something.

Or maybe I really did have jet lag, and that whole I-am-a-talentless-bum thing from yesterday wasn't rooted in my low self-esteem, but was due to a chemical imbalance from lack of REM. You know they say that people who are sleep deprived start suffering from hallucinations after a while. There was a DJ who stayed up for eleven days straight, the longest recorded period of time anyone has ever gone without sleep, and he started playing nothing but Phil Collins, and that's how they knew it was time to call the ambulance.

Except that even after fifteen hours of sleep, I still feel like a bit of a talentless bum. But at least today

I don't feel like it's such a tragedy. I think sleeping for fifteen hours straight has given me some perspective. I mean, not everyone can be super geniuses like Lilly and Michael. Just like not everyone can be a violin virtuoso like Boris. I have to be good at *something*. I just need to figure out what that something is. I asked Mr. G today at breakfast what he thinks I am good at, and he said he thinks I make some interesting fashion statements sometimes.

But that cannot have been what Lilly was referring to, as I was wearing my school uniform at the time she mentioned my mystery talent, which hardly leaves room for creative expression.

Mr. G's remark reminded me that I still haven't found my Queen Amidala underwear. But I wasn't about to ask my stepfather if he'd seen them. EW! I try not to look at Mr. Gianini's underwear when it comes back all folded from the laundry-by-the-pound place, and thankfully he extends the same courtesy to me.

And I couldn't ask my mom because once again she was dead to the world this morning. I guess pregnant women need as much sleep as teenagers and DJs.

But I had seriously better find them before Friday, or my first date with Michael will be a full on disaster, I just know it. Like, he'll probably open his present and be all, "Uh . . . I guess it's the thought that counts."

I probably should have just followed Mrs. Hakim Baba's rules and gotten him a sweater.

But Michael is so not the sweater type! I realized it as we pulled up in front of his building today. He was standing there, looking all tall and manly and Heath Ledger-like . . . except for having dark hair, not blond.

And his scarf was kind of blowing in the wind, and I could see that part of his throat, you know, right beneath his Adam's apple and right above where his shirt collar opens, the part that Lars once told me if you hit someone hard enough, it would paralyze them. Michael's throat was so nice-looking, so smooth and concave, that all I could think about was Mr. Rochester, out on Mesrour, his horse, brooding about his great love for Jane. . . .

And I knew, I just knew, I was right not to have gotten Michael a sweater. I mean, Kate Bosworth would never have given her quarterback boyfriend a *sweater*. Ew.

Anyway, then Michael saw me and smiled and he didn't look like Mr. Rochester anymore, because Mr. Rochester never smiled.

He just looked like Michael. And my heart turned over in my chest like it always does when I see him.

"Are you okay?" he wanted to know, as soon as he got into the limo. His eyes, so brown they are almost black—like the peat bogs Mr. Rochester was always striding past out there on the moor, because if you step into a peat bog, you can sink in up to your head and never be heard from again . . . which in a way is like what happens every time I look into Michael's eyes: I fall and fall and am pretty sure I will never be able to get out of them again, but that's okay, because I love being there—looked deeply into mine. My eyes are merely gray, the color of a New York City sidewalk. Or parking meter.

"I called you last night," Michael said, as his sister pushed him to move over on the seat so that she could get into the limo, too. "But your mom said you'd passed out—"

"I was really, really tired," I said, delighted by the fact that he appeared to have been worried about me. "I slept for fifteen hours straight."

"Whatever," Lilly said. She was clearly not interested in the details of my sleep cycle. "I heard from the producers of your movie."

I was surprised. "Really? What did they say?"

"They asked me to take a breakfast meeting with them," Lilly said, sounding like she was trying not to brag. Only she wasn't succeeding terribly well. You could totally hear the gloating in her voice. "Friday morning. So I won't be needing a ride."

"Wow," I said, impressed. "A breakfast meeting? Really? Will they serve bagels?"

"Probably," Lilly said.

I was impressed. I have never been invited to a breakfast meeting with producers before. Just the

Genovian ambassador to Spain.

I asked Lilly if she had come up with a list of demands for the producers, and she said she had, but she wouldn't tell me what they were.

I think I am going to have to watch this movie, and see what's making her so mad. My mom has it on tape. She said it was one of the funniest things she has ever seen.

But then, my mom laughs all through *Dirty Dancing*, even the parts that aren't supposed to be funny, so I don't know if she is the best judge.

Uh-oh. One of the cheerleaders (sadly, not Lana) tore her Achilles tendon doing pilates over the break, so they just announced they are holding tryouts for a replacement, as the team's alternate got transferred to a girls' school in Massachusetts due to having too wild of a party while her parents were in Martinique.

I sincerely hope Lilly is too busy protesting the movie of my life to protest the new cheerleading try-outs. Last semester she made me walk around with a big sign that said CHEERLEADING IS SEXIST AND NOT A SPORT, which I am not even sure is technically true, since they have cheerleading championships on ESPN. But it is a fact that there are no cheerleaders for the female sports in our school. Like Lana and her gang never turn out for the girls' basketball team or the girls' volleyball team, but they never miss a boys' game. So maybe the sexist part is true.

Oh, God, a geek just came in with a hall pass. A hall pass for me! I am being summoned to the office! And I didn't even do anything! Well, not this time, anyway.

Wednesday, January 21,
Principal Gupta's office

I can't believe it is only the second day of second semester, and already I am sitting here in the principal's office. I might not have finished my homework, but I fully have a note from my stepdad. I turned it in to the administrative office first thing. It says:

> Please excuse Mia for not completing her homework for Tuesday, January 20. She was crippled with jet lag, and unable to attend to her academic responsibilities last evening. She will of course make up the work tonight.
>
> —Frank Gianini

It kind of sucks when your stepdad is also your teacher.

But why would Principal Gupta object to this? I mean, I realize it is only the second day of second semester, and already I've fallen behind. But I'm not *that* far behind.

And I haven't even seen Lana today, so it's not like I could have done anything to her or her personal belongings.

OH, MY GOD. It just occurred to me. What if they realize they made a mistake, putting me back in Gifted and Talented? I mean, because I have no gifts or talents? What if I was only put in there in the first place because of some computer glitch, and now they've corrected it, and they're going to put me in Tech Ed or Domestic Arts, where I belong? I will have to make a spice rack!!! Or worse, a western omelet!!!

And I will never see Michael anymore! Okay, I will see him on the way to school and during lunch and after school and on weekends and holidays, but that's it. By taking me out of Gifted and Talented class, they will be depriving me of five whole hours of Michael a week! And true, during class we don't talk all that much, because Michael really *is* gifted and talented, unlike me, and needs to use that class period to hone his musical abilities instead of tutoring me, which is what he generally ends up doing thanks to my uselessness at Algebra.

But still, at least we are *together*.

Oh, God, this is awful! If I really do turn out to have a talent—which I doubt—WHY didn't Lilly just tell me what it is? Then I could throw it in Principal Gupta's face when she tries to deport me back to Tech Ed.

Wait . . . who does that voice belong to? The one coming from Principal Gupta's office? It sounds kind of familiar. It sounds kind of like . . .

I cannot believe Grandmère just did this. I mean, what kind of person DOES this? Just yanks a teenager out of school like this?

She is supposed to be the adult. She is supposed to be setting a good example for me.

And what does she do instead?

Well, first she tells a big fat LIE, and *then* she removes me from school property under false pretenses.

I am telling you, if my mom or dad finds out about this, Clarisse Renaldo will be a dead woman.

And not like she didn't practically give me a heart attack, you know. Good thing my cholesterol and everything is so low thanks to my vegetarian diet, otherwise I might have suffered a serious cardial infarction, she scared me so bad, coming out of Principal Gupta's office like that and being all, "Well, yes, we are of course praying for his quick recovery, but you know how these things can be—"

I felt all the blood run out of my face at the sight of her. Not just because, you know, it was Grandmère, talking to Principal Gupta, of all people, but because of what she was saying.

I stood up fast, my heart pounding so hard, I thought it might go flying right out of my chest.

"What is it?" I asked, all panicky. "Is it my dad? Is

the cancer back? Is that it? You can tell me, I can take it."

I was sure, from the way Grandmère was talking to Principal Gupta, that my dad's testicular cancer was back, and that he was going to have to go through treatment for it all over again—

"I will tell you in the car," Grandmère said to me, stiffly. "Come along."

"No, really," I said, trailing after her, with Lars trailing after me. "You can tell me now. I can take it, I swear I can. Is Dad all right?"

"Don't worry about your homework, Mia," Principal Gupta called to us as we left her office. "You just concentrate on being there for your father."

So it was true! Dad *was* sick!

"Is it the cancer again?" I asked Grandmère as we left the school and headed down to her limo, which was parked out front by the stone lion that guards the steps up to Albert Einstein High. "Do the doctors think it's treatable? Does he need a bone marrow transplant? Because you know, we're probably a match, on account of my having his hair. At least, what his hair must have looked like, back when he had some."

It wasn't until we were safely inside the limo that Grandmère gave me a very disgusted look and said, "Really, Amelia. There is nothing wrong with your father. There is, however, something wrong with that school of yours. Imagine, not allowing their pupils any sort of absences except in the case of illness. Ridiculous! Sometimes, you know, people need a day. A personal day, I think they call it. Well, today, Amelia, is your personal day."

I blinked at her from my side of the limo. I couldn't quite believe what I was hearing.

"Wait a minute," I said. "You mean . . . Dad isn't sick?"

"*Pfuit!*" Grandmère said, her drawn-on eyebrows raised way up. "He certainly seemed healthy enough when I spoke to him this morning."

"Then what—" I stared at her. "Why did you tell Principal Gupta—"

"Because otherwise she would not have allowed you out of class," Grandmère said, glancing at her gold-and-diamond watch. "And we are late, as it is. Really, there is nothing worse than an overzealous educator. They think they are helping, when in reality, you know, there are many different varieties of learning. Not all of it takes place in a classroom."

Comprehension was beginning to dawn. Grandmère had not pulled me out of school in the middle of the day because anyone in my family was sick. No, Grandmère had pulled me out of school because she wanted to teach me something.

"Grandmère," I cried, hardly able to believe what I

was hearing. "You can't just drive over and yank me out of school whenever you want to. And you certainly can't tell Principal Gupta that my dad is sick when he isn't! How could you even *say* something like that? Don't you know anything about self-fulfilling prophecies? I mean, if you go around lying about stuff like that all the time, it could actually come true—"

"Don't be ridiculous, Amelia," Grandmère said. "Your father is not going to have to go back to the hospital just because I told a little white lie to an academic administrator."

"I don't know how you can be so sure of that," I said angrily. "And anyway, where do you think you're taking me? I can't afford to just be leaving school in the middle of the day, you know, Grandmère. I mean, I am not as smart as most of the other kids in my class, and I've got a lot of catching up to do, thanks to the fact that I went to bed so early last night—"

"Oh, I *am* sorry," Grandmère said, very sarcastically. "I know how much you enjoy your Algebra class. I am sure it is a very great deprivation to you, missing it today. . . ."

I couldn't deny that she was right. At least partially. While I wasn't all that thrilled about the method by which she'd done it, the fact that Grandmère had extracted me from Algebra wasn't exactly something I was about to cry over. I mean, come on. Integers are not my best thing.

"Well, wherever we're going," I said severely, "we better be back in time for lunch. Because Michael will wonder where I am—"

"Not *that boy* again," Grandmère said, lifting her gaze to the limo's sunroof with a sigh.

"Yes, *that boy*," I said. "That boy I happen to love with all of my heart and soul. And Grandmère, if you could just meet him, you'd know—"

"Oh, we're here," Grandmère said, with some relief, as her driver pulled over. "At last. Get out, Amelia."

I got out of the limo, then looked around to see where Grandmère had brought me. But all I saw was the big Chanel store on Fifty-seventh Street. But that couldn't be where we were headed. Could it?

But when Grandmère untangled Rommel from his Louis Vuitton leash, put him on the ground, and began striding purposefully toward those big glass doors, I saw that Chanel was exactly where we were headed.

"Grandmère," I cried, rushing after her. "Chanel? You pulled me out of class to take me *shopping?*"

"You need a gown," Grandmère said with a sniff, "for the black-and-white ball at the Contessa Trevanni's this Friday. This was the soonest I could get an appointment."

"Black-and-white ball?" I echoed as Lars escorted us into the hushed white interior of Chanel, the world's most exclusive fashion boutique—the kind of store that, before I found out I was a princess, I would have been too terrified even to set foot in . . . although I can't say the same for my friends, as Lilly once filmed an entire episode of her cable access show from inside a dressing room at Chanel. She'd barricaded herself in and was trying on Karl Lagerfeld's latest creations and wouldn't come out until security broke the door down and escorted her to the sidewalk. It had been a show on how haute couture designers are completely sizeist, seeing as how it is impossible to find leather pants in anything larger than a misses' size ten. "What black-and-white ball?"

"Surely your mother told you," Grandmère said, as a tall, reed-thin woman approached us with cries of, "Your Royal Highnesses! How delightful to see you."

"My mother didn't tell me anything about a ball," I said. "When did you say it was?"

"Friday night," Grandmère said to me. To the saleslady she said, "Yes, I believe you've put aside some gowns for my granddaughter. I specifically requested white ones." Grandmère blinked owlishly at me. "You are too young for black. I don't want to hear any arguing about it."

Argue about it? How could I argue about something I hadn't even begun to understand?

"Of course," the saleslady was saying with a big smile. "Come with me, won't you, Your Highness?"

"Friday night?" I cried, that part, at least, of what

was going on beginning to sink in. "Friday night? Grandmère, I can't go to any ball on Friday night. I already made plans with—"

But Grandmère just put her hand in the center of my back and pushed.

And then I was tripping after the saleslady, who didn't even blink an eye, as if princesses in combat boots go tripping after her all the time.

And now I am sitting in Grandmère's limo on my way back to school, and all I can think about are the number of people I would like to thank for my current predicament, foremost among which is my mother, for forgetting to tell me that she had already given Grandmère permission to drag me to this thing; the Contessa Trevanni, for having a black-and-white ball in the first place; the salespeople at Chanel, who, although they are very nice, are really all just a bunch of enablers, as they have enabled my grandma to garb me in a white diamante ball gown and drag me to something I have no desire to attend in the first place; my father, for setting his mother loose upon the helpless city of Manhattan without anyone to supervise her; and of course Grandmère herself, for completely ruining my life.

Because when I told her, while the Chanel people were throwing yards of fabric over me, that I cannot possibly attend Contessa Trevanni's black-and-white ball this Friday night, as that is the night Michael and

I are supposed to have our first date, she responded by giving me a big lecture about how a princess's first duty is to her people. Her heart, Grandmère says, must always come second.

I tried to explain how this date could not be postponed or rescheduled, as *Star Wars* would only be showing at the Screening Room that night, and that after that they would go back to showing *Moulin Rouge*, which I won't see because I heard someone dies at the end.

But Grandmère refused to see that my date with Michael was anywhere near as important as Contessa Trevanni's black-and-white ball. Apparently Contessa Trevanni is a very socially prominent member of the Monaco royal family, besides being some kind of distant cousin (who isn't?) of ours. My not attending her black-and-white ball here in the city with all the other debutantes would be a slight from which the royal house of Grimaldi might never recover.

I pointed out that my not attending *Star Wars* with Michael will be a slight from which my relationship with my boyfriend might never recover. But Grandmère said only that if Michael really loves me, he'll understand when I have to cancel on him.

"And if he doesn't," Grandmère said, exhaling a plume of gray smoke from the Gitanes she was sucking down, "then he was never appropriate consort material to begin with."

Which is very easy for Grandmère to say. *She* hasn't been in love with Michael since the first grade. *She* doesn't spend hours and hours attempting to write poems befitting his greatness. *She* doesn't know what it is to love, since the only person Grandmère has ever been in love with in her entire life is herself.

Well, it's true.

And now we are pulling up to the school. It is lunchtime. In a minute I will have to go inside and explain to Michael how I cannot make it to our first date, or it will cause an international incident from which the country over which I will one day rule may never recover.

Why couldn't Grandmère just have sent me to boarding school in Massachusetts instead?

Wednesday, January 21, G & T

I couldn't tell him.

I mean, how could I? Especially when he was being so nice to me during lunch. Everybody in the whole school, it seemed, knew that Grandmère had come and taken me away during homeroom. In her chinchilla cape, with those eyebrows, and Rommel at her side, how could anyone have missed her? She is as conspicuous as Cher.

Everyone was all concerned, you know, about the supposed illness in my family. Michael especially. He was all, "Is there anything I can do? Your Algebra homework, or something? I know it isn't much, but it's the least I could do. . . ."

How could I tell him the truth—that my father wasn't sick; that my grandmother had dragged me off in the middle of school to take me *shopping*? Shopping for a dress to wear at a ball to which he was not invited, and which was to take place during the exact time we were supposed to be enjoying dinner and a space fantasy set in a galaxy far, far away?

I couldn't. I couldn't tell him. I couldn't tell anyone. I just sat there at lunch being all quiet. People mistook my lack of talkativeness for extreme mental distress. Which it was, actually, only not for the reasons they thought. Basically all I was thinking as I sat there was I HATE MY GRANDMOTHER. I HATE

MY GRANDMOTHER. I HATE MY GRAND-
MOTHER. I HATE MY GRANDMOTHER.

I really, really do.

As soon as lunch was over, I snuck off to one of the
pay phones outside the auditorium doors and called
home. I knew my mom would be there instead of at her
studio because she is still working on the nursery walls.
She'd gotten to the third wall, on which she was depict-
ing a highly realistic painting of the fall of Saigon.

"Oh, Mia," she said, when I asked her if there
wasn't something she'd possibly forgotten to mention
to me. "I am so sorry. Your grandmother called during
Anna Nicole. You know how I get during *Anna Nicole*."

"Mom," I said through gritted teeth. "Why did you
tell her it was okay for me to go to this stupid thing?
You told me I could go out with Michael that night!"

"I did?" My mom sounded bewildered. And why
shouldn't she have? She clearly did not remember the
conversation she'd had with me about my date with
Michael . . . primarily of course because she'd been
dead to the world during it. Still, she didn't need to
know that. What was important was that she was made
to feel as guilty as possible for the heinous crime she
had committed. "Oh, honey. I am so sorry. Well,
you're just going to have to cancel with Michael. He'll
understand."

"Mom," I cried. "He will not! This was supposed
to be our first real date! You've got to do something!"

"Well," my mom said, sounding kind of wry. "I'm a little surprised to hear you're so unhappy about it, sweetheart. You know, considering your whole thing about not wanting to chase Michael. Canceling your first date with him would definitely fall into that category."

"Very funny, Mom," I said. "But Jane wouldn't cancel her first date with Mr. Rochester. She just wouldn't call him all the time beforehand, or let him get to second base during it."

"Oh," my mom said.

"Look," I said. "This is serious. You've got to get me out of this stupid ball!"

But all my mom said was that she'd talk to my dad about it. I knew what that meant, of course. No way was I getting out of this ball. My dad has never in his life forsaken duty for love. He is full-on Princess Margaret that way.

So now I've been sitting here (trying to do my Algebra homework, as usual, because I am neither gifted nor talented), knowing that at some point or another I am going to have to tell Michael our date is canceled. Only how? How am I going to do it? And what if he's so mad, he never asks me out again?

Worse, what if he asks some other girl to see *Star Wars* with him? I mean, some girl who knows all the lines you're supposed to shout at the screen during the movie. Like when Ben Kenobi goes, "Obi-Wan. Now that's a name I haven't heard in a long time," you're supposed to shout, "How long?" and then Ben goes, "A very long time."

There must be a million girls besides me who know about this. Michael could ask any one of them instead of me and have a perfectly wonderful time. Without me.

Lilly is bugging me to find out what's wrong. She keeps passing me notes, because they are fumigating the teachers' lounge, so Mrs. Hill is in here today, pretending to grade papers from her fourth-period computer class. But really she is ordering things from a Garnet Hill catalog. I saw it beneath her gradebook.

Is your dad super sick? Lilly's latest note reads. *Are you going to have to fly back to Genovia?*

No, I write back.

Is it the cancer? Lilly wants to know. *Did he have a recurrence?*

No, I write back.

Well, what is it, then? Lilly's handwriting is getting spiky, a sure sign she is becoming impatient with me. *Why won't you tell me?*

Because, I want to scrawl back, in big capital letters. *The truth will lead to the imminent demise of my romantic relationship with your brother, and I couldn't bear that! Don't you see I can't live without him?*

But I can't write that, because I'm not ready to give up yet. I mean, am I not a princess of the royal house of Renaldo? Do princesses of the royal house of

Renaldo just give up, just like that, when something they hold as dearly as I hold Michael is at stake?

No, they do not. Look at my ancestresses, Agnes and Rosagunde. Agnes jumped off a bridge in order to get what she wanted (not be a nun). And Rosagunde strangled a guy with her own hair (in order to not have to sleep with him). Was I, Mia Thermopolis, going to let a little thing like the Contessa Trevanni's black-and-white ball get in the way of my having my first date with the man I love?

No, I was not.

Perhaps this, then, is my talent. The indomitability that I inherited from the Renaldo princesses before me.

Struck by this realization, I wrote a hasty note to Lilly:

Is my talent that I, like my ancestresses before me, am indomitable?

I waited breathlessly for her response. Although it was not clear to me what I was going to do if she replied in the positive. Because what kind of talent is being indomitable? I mean, you can't get paid for it, the way you can if your talent is playing the violin or songwriting or producing cable access television programs.

Still, it would be good to know I'd figured out my talent on my own. You know, as far as climbing the Jungian tree to self-actualization went.

But Lilly's response was way disappointing:

No, your talent is not that you're indomitable, dinkus.

God, U R so dense sometimes. WHAT IS WRONG WITH YOUR DAD?????

Sighing, I realized I had no choice but to write back, *Nothing. Grandmère just wanted to take me to Chanel, so she made up the thing about my dad being sick.*

God, Lilly wrote back. *No wonder you're looking like you ate a sock again. Your grandmother sucks.*

I could not agree more. If only Lilly knew the full extent of how much.

Wednesday, January 21, sixth period, third-floor stairwell

Emergency meeting of the followers of the Jane Eyre technique of boyfriend-handling. We are of course in peril of discovery at any moment, as we are skipping French in order to gather here in the stairwell leading to the roof (the door to which is locked, of course: Lilly says in the movie of my life, the kids got to go on the roof of their school all the time. Just another example of how art most certainly does not imitate life), so that we can lend succor to one of our sisters in suffering.

That's right. It turns out that I am not the only one for whom the semester is off to an inauspicious beginning. Not only did Tina sprain her ankle on the ski slopes of Aspen—no, she also got a text message from Dave Farouq El-Abar during fifth period over her new cell phone. It said, U NEVER CALLED BACK. AM TAKING JASMINE TO RANGER GAME. HAVE A NICE LIFE.

I have never in my life seen anything so insensitive as that message. I swear, my blood went cold as I read it.

"Sexist pig," Lilly said when she saw it. "Don't even worry about it, Tina. You'll find somebody better."

"I d-don't want someone b-better." Tina sobbed. "I only want D-Dave!"

It breaks my heart to see her in such pain—not just emotional pain, either: it was no joke trying to get up to the third-floor stairwell on her crutches. I have promised faithfully to sit with her while she works through her anguish (Lilly is taking her through Elisabeth Kübler-Ross's five stages of break-up grief: Denial—I can't believe he would do this to me; Anger—Jasmine is probably a cow who Frenches on the first date; Bargaining—maybe if I tell him I'll call him faithfully every night, he'll take me back; Depression—I'll never love another man again; Acceptance—well, I guess he *was* kind of selfish). Of course being here with Tina, instead of in French class, means I am risking possible suspension, which is the penalty for skipping class here at Albert Einstein.

But what is more important, my disciplinary record, or my friend?

Besides, Lars is keeping a lookout at the bottom of the stairs. If Mr. Kreblutz, the head custodian, comes along, Lars is going to whistle the Genovian anthem, and we'll flatten ourselves against the wall by the old gym mats (which are quite smelly, by the way, and undoubtedly a fire hazard).

Although I am deeply saddened for her, I can't help feeling that Tina's situation has taught me a valuable lesson: that the Jane Eyre technique of boyfriend-handling is not necessarily the most reliable method by which to hang on to your boyfriend.

Except that, according to Grandmère, who did manage to hang on to a husband for forty years, the quickest way to turn a guy off is to chase after him.

And certainly Lilly, who has the longest-running relationship of any of us, does not chase after Boris. Really, if anything, *he* is the one doing the chasing. But that is probably because Lilly is too busy with her various lawsuits and projects to pay much more than perfunctory attention to him.

Somewhere between the two of them—Grandmère and Lilly—must lie the truth to maintaining a successful relationship with a man. Somehow I have got to get the hang of this, because I will tell you one thing: if I ever get a message from Michael like the one Tina just got from Dave, I will fully be taking a swan dive off the Tappan Zee. And I highly doubt any cute coast guard captain is going to come along and fish me out—at least, not in one piece. The Tappan Zee Bridge is *way* higher than the Pont des Vierges.

And of course you know what this means—this whole thing with Tina and Dave, I mean. It means that I can't cancel my date with Michael. No way, nohow. I don't care if Monaco starts lobbing SCUD missiles at the Genovian House of Parliament: I am not going to that black-and-white ball. Grandmère and the Contessa Trevanni are just going to have to learn how to live with disappointment.

Because when it comes to our men, we Renaldo women don't mess around. We play for keeps.

HOMEWORK

Algebra: probs at beginning of Ch. 11,
PLUS . . . ??? Don't know, thanks to Grandmère
English: update journal (How I Spent My Winter
Break—500 words), PLUS . . . ??? Don't know,
thanks to Grandmère
Bio: read Chapter 13, PLUS . . . ??? Don't know,
thanks to Grandmère
Health and Safety: Chapter 1, You and Your
Environment, PLUS . . . ??? Don't know, thanks
to Grandmère
G & T: figure out secret talent
French: Chapitre Dix, PLUS . . . Don't know,
due to skipping!!!!
World Civ: Chapter 13: Brave New World; bring
in current event illustrating how technology can
cost society

Wednesday, January 21, limo on the way home from Grandmère's

While I might never actually figure out what my own talent is—if I even have one—Grandmère's is only too painfully obvious. Clarisse Renaldo has a total gift for completely destroying my life. It is abundantly clear to me now that this has been her goal all along. The simple fact of the matter is, Grandmère can't stand Michael. Not, of course, because he's ever done anything to her. Never done anything to her except make her granddaughter superbly, sublimely happy. She's never even met him.

No, Grandmère doesn't like Michael because Michael is not royal.

How do I know this? Well, it became pretty obvious when I walked into her suite for my princess lesson today, and who should just be coming in from his racquetball game at the New York Athletic Club, swinging his racquet and looking all Andre Agassi-ish? Oh, only Prince René.

"What are YOU doing here?" I demanded in a manner that Grandmère later reproved me for (she said my question was unladylike in its accusatory tone, as if I suspected René of something underhanded, which, of course, I did. I practically had to beat him over the head back in Genovia to get my scepter back).

"Enjoying your beautiful city," was how René

replied. And then he excused himself to go shower, because, as he put it, he was a bit ripe from the court.

"Really, Amelia," Grandmère said, disapprovingly. "Is that any way to greet your cousin?"

"Why isn't he back in school?" I wanted to know.

"For your information," Grandmère said, "he happens to be on a break."

"Still?" This sounds pretty suspicious to me. I mean, what kind of business college—even a French one—has a Christmas break that goes practically into February?

"Schools like René's," was Grandmère's explanation for this, "traditionally have a longer winter holiday than American ones, so that their pupils can make full use of the ski season."

"I didn't see any skis on him," I pointed out craftily.

"Pfuit!" was all Grandmère had to say about it, however. "René has had enough of the slopes this year. Besides, he adores Manhattan."

Well, I guess I could see that. I mean, New York *is* the greatest city in the world, after all. Why, just the other day, a construction worker down on Forty-second Street found a twenty-pound rat! That's a rat that's only five pounds lighter than my cat! You won't be finding any twenty-pound rats in Paris or Hong Kong, that's for sure.

So, anyway, we were going along, doing the princess-lesson thing—you know, Grandmère was instructing me about all the personages I was going to meet at this black-and-white ball, including this year's crop of debutantes, the daughters of socialites and other so-called American royalty, who were "coming out" to Society with a capital S, and looking for husbands (even though what they should be looking for, if you ask me, is a good undergraduate program, and maybe a part-time job teaching illiterate homeless people to read. But that's just me.) when all of a sudden, it occurred to me, the solution to my problem:

Why couldn't Michael be my escort to the Contessa Trevanni's black-and-white ball?

Okay, granted, it was no *Star Wars*. And yeah, he'd have to get his hands on a tux and all. But at least we would be together. At least I could still give him his birthday present in a forum that was outside of the cinderblock walls of Albert Einstein High. At least I wouldn't have to cancel on him altogether. At least the state of diplomatic affairs between Genovia and Monaco would remain at DefCon Five.

But how, I wondered, was I ever going to get Grandmère to go along with it? I mean, she hadn't said anything about the Contessa letting me bring a date.

Still, what about all those debutantes? Weren't they bringing dates? Wasn't that what West Point Military Academy was *for*? Providing dates to debutante balls? And if those girls could bring dates, and they weren't even princesses, why couldn't I?

How I was going to get Grandmère to let me bring Michael to the black-and-white ball, after all of our long discussions about how you mustn't let the object of your affection even know that you like him, was going to be a major obstacle. I decided I would have to exercise some of the diplomatic tact Grandmère had taken so much trouble to teach me.

"And please, whatever else you do, Amelia," Grandmère was saying, as she sat there running a hair-pick through Rommel's sparse fur, as the royal Genovian vet had instructed, "do not stare too long at the Contessa's face-lift. I know it will be difficult—it looks as if the surgeon botched it horribly. But actually, it's exactly the way Elena wanted it to look. Apparently she has always fancied resembling a walleyed bass—"

"Listen, about this dance, Grandmère," I started in, all subtly. "Do you think the Contessa would mind if I, you know . . . brought someone?"

Grandmère looked at me confusedly over Rommel's pink, trembling body. "What do you mean? Amelia, I highly doubt your mother would have a very nice time at the Contessa Trevanni's black-and-white ball. For one thing, there won't be any other hippy radicals there—"

"Not my mom," I said, realizing that perhaps I had been a little too subtle. "I was thinking more, you know. Of an escort."

"But you already have an escort." Grandmère

adjusted Rommel's diamond-flake-encrusted collar.

"I do?" I did not recall asking anyone to scrounge up a West Pointer for me.

"Of course you do," Grandmère said, still not, I noticed, meeting my gaze. "Prince René has very generously offered to serve as your escort to the ball. Now, where were we? Oh, yes. About the Contessa's taste in clothes. I think you've learned enough by now to know that you aren't to comment—at least to her face—on what any of your hostesses happen to be wearing. But I think it necessary to warn you that the Contessa has a tendency to wear clothes that are somewhat young on her, and that reveal—"

"*René* is going to be my escort?" I stood up, nearly knocking Grandmère's Sidecar over as I did so. "*René* is taking me to the black-and-white ball?"

"Well, yes," Grandmère said, looking blandly innocent—a little too blandly innocent, if you asked me. "He is, after all, a guest in this city—in this country, as a matter of fact. I would think that you, Amelia, would be only too happy to make him feel welcome and wanted—"

I narrowed my eyes at her. "What is going on here?" I demanded. "Grandmère, are you trying to fix up René and me?"

"Certainly not," Grandmère said, looking genuinely appalled by the suggestion. But then, I'd been fooled by Grandmère's expressions before. Especially the one she puts on when she wants you to think that she is just a helpless old lady. "Your imagination most definitely comes from your mother's side of the family. Your father was never as fanciful as you are, Amelia, for which I can only thank God. He'd have driven me to an early grave, I'm convinced of it, if he'd been half as capricious as you tend to be, young lady."

"Well, what else am I supposed to think?" I asked, feeling a little sheepish over my outburst. After all, the idea that Grandmère might, even though I was only fourteen, be trying to fix me up with some prince that she wanted me to marry *was* a little outlandish. I mean, even for Grandmère. "You made us dance together—"

"For a magazine pictorial." Grandmère sniffed.

"—and then your not liking Michael—"

"I never said I didn't like him. From what I know of him, I think he is a perfectly charming boy. I just want you to be realistic about the fact that you, Amelia, are not like other girls. You are a princess, and have the good of your country to think of."

"—and then René showing up like this, and you're announcing he's taking me to the black-and-white ball—"

"Is it wrong of me to want to see the poor boy have a nice time while he is here? He has suffered so many hardships, losing his ancestral home, not to mention his own kingdom—"

"Grandmère," I said. "René wasn't even alive when

they kicked his family out—"

"All the more reason," Grandmère said, "you should be sensitive to his plight."

Great. What am I supposed to do now? About Michael, I mean? I can't bring both him *and* Prince René to the ball. I mean, I look weird enough, with my half-grown-out hair and my androgyny (although judging by Grandmère's description of her, the Contessa might look even weirder than I do) without hauling two dates and a bodyguard around with me.

I wish I were Princess Leia instead of me, Princess Mia. I'd *so* rather take on the Death Star than a black-and-white ball.

Wednesday, January 21, the loft

Well, my mom getting hold of my dad about the Contessa's ball was a washout. Apparently the whole parking-meter debate has gotten way out of control. The minister of tourism is conducting a filibuster of his own, in response to the one from the minister of finance, and there can't be a vote until he stops talking and sits down. So far he's been talking for twelve hours, forty-eight minutes. I don't know why my dad doesn't just have him arrested and put in the dungeon.

I am really starting to be afraid that I am not going to be able to get out of this ball thingie.

"You better let Michael know," my mom just poked her head in to say, helpfully. "That you won't be able to make it Friday. Hey, are you writing in your journal again? Aren't you supposed to be doing your homework?"

Trying to change the subject from my homework (hello, I am totally doing it, I am just taking a break right now), I went, "Mom, I am not saying anything to Michael until we've heard from Dad. Because there's no point in my running the risk of Michael breaking up with me if Dad's just going to turn around and say I don't have to go to the stupid ball."

"Mia," my mom said. "Michael is not going to break up with you just because you have a familial commitment you cannot get out of."

"I wouldn't be so sure," I said darkly. "Dave Farouq El-Abar broke up with Tina today because she didn't return his call."

"That's different," my mom said. "It's just plain rude not to return someone's calls."

"But Mom," I said. I was getting tired of having to explain this stuff to my mom all the time. It is a wonder to me she ever got a single guy in the first place, let alone two of them, when she clearly knows so little about the art of dating. "If you are too available, the guy might think all the thrill has gone out of the chase."

My mother looked suspicious. "Don't tell me. Let me guess. Your grandmother told you that?"

"Um," I said. "Yes."

"Well, let me give you a little tip my mother once gave me," my mom said. I was surprised. My mom doesn't get along so well with her parents, so it is rare that she mentions either of them ever giving her a piece of advice worthy of passing down to her own daughter.

"If you think there's a chance you might have to cancel on Michael for Friday night," she said, "you'd better cat-on-the-roof him now."

I was understandably perplexed by this. "Cat on the whatta?"

"Cat on the roof," my mother said. "You need to begin mentally preparing him for the disappointment. For instance, if something had happened to Fat Louie while you were in Genovia—" My mouth must have fallen open, since my mom went, "Don't worry, nothing did. But I'm just saying, if something had, I would not just have blurted it right out to you, over the phone. I'd have prepared you gently for the eventual letdown. Like I might have said, 'Mia, Fat Louie escaped through your window, and now he's up on the roof, and we can't get him down.'"

"Of course you could get him down," I protested. "You could go up by the fire escape and take a pillowcase and when you get near him, you could throw the pillowcase over him and scoop him up and carry him back down again."

"Yes," my mom said. "But supposing I told you I'd try that. And the next day I called you and said it hadn't worked, Fat Louie had escaped to the neighbor's roof—"

"I'd tell you to go to the building next door and make someone let you in, then go up to their roof." I really did not see where this was going. "Mom, how could you be so irresponsible as to let Fat Louie out in the first place? I've told you again and again, you've got to keep my bedroom window closed, you know how he likes to watch the pigeons. Louie doesn't have any outdoor survival skills—"

"So naturally," my mom said, "you wouldn't expect him to survive two nights out of doors."

"No," I practically wailed. "I wouldn't."

"Right. See. So you'd be mentally prepared when I called you on the third day to say despite everything we'd done, Louie was dead."

"OH, MY GOD!" I snatched up Fat Louie from where he was lying beside me on the bed. "And you think I should do that to poor Michael? He has a dog, not a cat! Pavlov's never going to get up on the roof!"

"No," my mother said, looking tired. Well, and why not? Her life's essence was being slowly devoured by the insatiable fetus growing inside her. "I'm saying you should begin mentally preparing Michael for the disappointment he is going to feel if indeed you need to cancel on him Friday night. Call him and tell him you might not be able to make it. That's all. Cat-on-the-roof him."

I let Fat Louie go. Not just because I finally realized what my mom was getting at, but because he was trying to bite me in order to get me to loosen the stranglehold I had on him.

"Oh," I said. "You think if I do that—start mentally preparing him for my not being able to go out with him on Friday—he won't dump me when I get around to breaking the actual news?"

"Mia," my mom said. "No boy is going to dump you because you have to cancel a date. If any boy does, then he wasn't worth going out with anyway. Much like Tina's Dave, I'd venture to say. She's probably better off without him. Now, do your homework."

Only how could anyone expect me to do my homework after receiving a piece of information like that?

Instead I went online. I meant to instant message Michael, but instead, I found that Tina was instant messaging me.

ILUVROMANCE: Hi, Mia. What R U doing?

She sounded so sad! She was even using a blue font!

FTLOUIE: I'm just doing my Bio. How are you?

ILUVROMANCE: OK, I guess. I just miss him so much!!!!!!!!!!!!!!!!!!!! I wish I had never even heard of stupid Jane Eyre.

Remembering what my mom had said, I wrote

FTLOUIE: Tina, if Dave was willing to break up with you just because you didn't return his calls, then he was not worthy of you. You will find a new boy, one who appreciates you.

ILUVROMANCE: Do U really think so?

FTLOUIE: Absolutely.

ILUVROMANCE: But where am I going to find a boy who appreC8s me at AEHS? All the boys who go there are morons. Except MM of course.

FtLouie: Don't worry, we'll find someone for you. I have to go IM my dad now—

I didn't want to tell her that the person I really had to IM was Michael. I didn't want to rub it in that I had a boyfriend and she didn't. Also, I hoped she didn't remember that in Genovia, where my dad was, it was four o'clock in the morning. Also that the Palais de Genovia isn't exactly state-of-the-art, technologically speaking.

FtLouie: —so TTYL.

ILuvRomance: OK, bye. If U feel like chatting later, I'll be here. I have nowhere else to go.

Poor, sweet Tina! She is clearly prostrate with grief. Really, if you think about it, she is well rid of Dave. If he wanted to leave her for this Jasmine girl so badly, he could have let her down gently by cat-on-the-roofing her. If he was any kind of gentleman, he would have. But it was all too clear now that Dave was no gentleman at all.

I'm glad *my* boyfriend is different. Or at least, I hope he is. No, wait—of course he is. He's MICHAEL.

FtLouie: Hey!

LINUXRULZ: Hey back atcha! Where have you been?

FTLOUIE: Princess lessons.

LINUXRULZ: Don't you know everything there is to know about being a princess yet?

FTLOUIE: Apparently not. Grandmère's got me in for some fine tuning. Speaking of which, is there, like, a later showing of *Star Wars* than the seven o'clock?

LINUXRULZ: Yeah, there's an eleven. Why?

FTLOUIE: Oh, nothing.

LINUXRULZ: WHY?

But see here was the part where I couldn't do it. Maybe because of the capital letters, or maybe because my conversation with Tina was still too fresh in my mind. The unparalleled sadness in her blue *U*s was just too much for me. I know I should have just come right out and told him about the ball thingie right then and there, only I couldn't go through with it. All I could think about was how incredibly smart and gifted Michael is, and what a pathetic talentless freak I am, and how easy it would be for him to go out and find someone worthier of his attentions.

So instead, I wrote

FTLOUIE: I've been trying to think of some names for your band.

LINUXRULZ: What does that have to do with whether or not there's a later showing of *Star Wars* Friday night?

FTLOUIE: Well, nothing, I guess. Except what do you think of Michael and the Wookiees?

LINUXRULZ: I think maybe you've been playing with Fat Louie's catnip mouse again.

FTLOUIE: Ha ha. OK, how about the Ewoks?

LINUXRULZ: The EWOKS? Where did your grandma take you today when she hauled you out of homeroom? Electric shock therapy?

FTLOUIE: I'm only trying to help.

LINUXRULZ: I know, sorry. Only I don't think the guys would really enjoy being equated with furry little muppets from the planet Endor. I mean, I know one of them is Boris, but even he would draw the line at Ewoks, I hope—

FTLOUIE: BORIS PELKOWSKI IS IN YOUR BAND????

LINUXRULZ: Yeah. Why?

FTLOUIE: Nothing.

All I can say is, if I had a band, I would not let Boris in it. I mean, I know he is a talented musician and all, but he is also a mouth breather. I think it's great that he and Lilly get along so great, and for short periods of time, I can totally put up with him and even have a nice time with him and all. But I would not let him be in my band. Not unless he stopped tucking his sweaters into his pants.

LINUXRULZ: Boris isn't so bad, once you get to know him.

FTLOUIE: I know. He just doesn't seem like the band type. All that Bartok.

LINUXRULZ: He plays a mean bluegrass, you know. Not that we'll be playing any bluegrass in the band.

This was comforting to know.

LINUXRULZ: So will your grandmother let you off on time?

I genuinely had no idea what he was talking about.

FTLOUIE: What????

LinuxRulz: On Friday. You've got princess lessons, right? That's why you were asking about later showings of the movie, wasn't it? You're worried your grandmother isn't going to let you out on time?

This is where I screwed up. You see, he had offered me the perfect out—I could have said, "Yes, I am," and chances were, he'd have been like, "Okay, well, let's make it another time, then."

BUT WHAT IF THERE WERE NO OTHER TIME????

What if Michael, like Dave, just blew me off and found some other girl to take to the show????

So instead, I went

FtLouie: No, it will be okay. I think I can get off early.

WHY AM I SO STUPID???? WHY DID I WRITE THAT???? Because of COURSE I won't be able to get off early, I will be at the stupid black-and-white ball ALL NIGHT!!!!!

I swear, I am such an idiot, I don't even deserve to have a boyfriend.

Thursday, January 22, Homeroom

This morning at breakfast, Mr. G was all, "Has anyone seen my brown corduroy pants?" and my mom, who had set her alarm so that she could wake up early enough to possibly catch my dad on a break between Parliament sessions (no such luck) went, "No, but has anyone seen my Free Winona T-shirt?"

And then I went, "Well, I still haven't found my Queen Amidala underwear."

And that's when we all realized it: Someone had stolen our laundry.

It is really the only explanation for it. I mean, we send our laundry out to the Thompson Street laundry-by-the-pound place, and then they do it for us and deliver it all folded and stuff. Since we don't have a doorman, generally the bag just sits in the vestibule until one of us picks it up and drags it up the three flights of stairs to the loft.

Only apparently no one has seen the bag of laundry we dropped off the day before I left for Genovia! (I guess I am the only one in my family who pays attention to things like laundry—clearly because I am the talentless one, and have nothing deeper to think about than clean underwear.)

Which can only mean that one of those freaky news reporters (who regularly go through our garbage, much to the chagrin of Mr. Molina, our building's superintendent) found our bag of laundry, and any minute we can expect a groundbreaking news story on the front cover of the *Post*: OUT OF THE CLOSET: WHAT PRINCESS MIA WEARS, AND WHAT IT MEANS, ACCORDING TO OUR EXPERTS.

AND THEN THE WHOLE WORLD WILL FIND OUT THAT I WEAR QUEEN AMIDALA PANTIES!

I mean, it is not like I go around *advertising* that I have *Star Wars* underwear, or even that I have any kind of lucky panties at all. And by rights, I should have taken my Queen Amidala underwear with me to Genovia, for luck on my Christmas Eve address to my people. If I had, maybe I wouldn't have gone off on that parking-meter tangent.

But whatever, I had been too caught up in the whole Michael thing, and had completely forgotten.

And now it looks like someone has gotten hold of my special lucky underwear, and the next thing you know, it will be showing up on eBay! Seriously! Who is to say a pair of my panties wouldn't sell like hotcakes? Especially the fact that they are Queen Amidala panties.

I am so, so dead.

Mom has already called the Sixth Precinct to report the theft, but those guys are too busy tracking down real criminals to go after a laundry swiper. They practically laughed her off the phone.

It is all very well for her and Mr. G; all they lost were regular clothes. I am the only one who lost underwear. Worse, my lucky underwear. I fully understand that the men and women who fight crime in this city have more important things to do than look for my underwear.

But the way things have been going, I really, really need all the good luck I can get.

Thursday, January 22, Algebra

THINGS TO DO

1. Have Genovian ambassador to the UN call the CIA. See if they can dispatch some agents to track down my underwear (if it falls into the wrong hands, there could be an international incident!).

2. Get cat food!!!!!

3. Check on Mom's folic acid intake.

4. Tell Michael I will not be able to make first date with him.

5. Prepare to be dumped.

<u>Defn</u>: Square root of perfect sq is either of the identical factors.
<u>Defn</u>: Positive sq root is called the principle sq root. Negative numbers have no sq root.

Thursday, January 22, Health and Safety

Did you see that? They are meeting at Cosi for lunch!

Yes. He so loves her.

It's so cute when teachers are in love.

So are you nervous about your breakfast meeting tomorrow?

Hardly. THEY are the ones who should be nervous.

Are you going all by yourself? Your mom and dad aren't going with you, are they?

Please. I can handle a bunch of movie executives on my own, thanks. How can they keep stuffing this infantile swill down our throats, year after year? Don't they think we know by now that tobacco kills? Hey, did you get all your homework done, or were you up all night IMing my brother instead?

Both.

You two are so cute, it makes me want to puke. Almost as cute as Mr. Wheeton and Mademoiselle Klein.

Shut up.

God, this is boring. Want to make another list?

Okay, you start.

LILLY MOSCOVITZ'S GUIDE TO
WHAT'S HOT AND WHAT'S NOT ON TV
(with commentary by Mia Thermopolis)

7th Heaven

*Lilly: A complex look at one family's struggles to maintain
christian mores in an ever-evolving, modern-day society.
Fairly well acted and occasionally moving, this show can
turn "preachy," but does depict the problems facing normal
families with surprising realism, and only occasionally sinks
to the banal.*

Mia: Even though the dad is a minister and everyone
has to learn a lesson at the end of every episode, this
show is pretty good. High point: When the Olsen
twins guest starred. Low point: When the show's
cosmetologist gave the youngest girl straight hair.

Popstars

*Lilly: A ridiculous attempt to pander to the lowest common
denominator, this show puts its young stars through a*

humiliatingly public "audition," then zeroes in as the losers cry and winners gloat.

Mia: They take a bunch of attractive people who can sing and dance and make them audition for a place in a pop group, and some of them get it and some of them don't, and the ones who do are instant celebrities who then crack up, all while wearing interesting and generally navel-baring outfits. How could this show be bad?

Sabrina the Teenage Witch

Lilly: Though based on comic-book characters, this show is surprisingly affable, and even occasionally amusing. Although, sadly, actual Wiccan practices are not described. The show could benefit from some research into the ages-old religion that has, through the centuries, empowered millions, primarily females. The talking cat is a bit suspect: I have not read any believable documentation that would support the possibility of transfiguration.

Mia: Totally awesome during the high school/Harvey years. Good-bye Harvey = good-bye show.

Baywatch

Lilly: Puerile garbage.

Mia: Most excellent show of all time. Everyone is good-looking; you can fully follow every plotline even while instant messaging; and there are lots of pictures of the beach, which is great when you are in dark, gloomy Manhattan in February. Best episode: When Pamela Anderson got kidnapped by that half man/half beast, who after plastic surgery became a professor at UCLA. Worst episode: Anytime Mitch adopts a son.

Powerpuff Girls

Lilly: Best show on television.

Mia: Ditto. 'Nough said.

Roswell

Lilly: Now, sadly, canceled, this show offered an intriguing look at the possibility that aliens live among us. The fact that they might be teenagers, and extraordinarily attractive ones, at that, stretches the show's credibility somewhat.

Mia: Hot guys with alien powers. What more can you ask? High point: Future Max; any time anybody made out in the eraser room. Low point: When that skanky Tess showed up. Oh, and when it got canceled.

Buffy the Vampire Slayer

Lilly: Feminist empowerment at its peak, entertainment at its best. The heroine is a lean, mean, vampire-killing machine, who worries as much about her immortal soul as she does about messing up her hair. A strong role model for young women—nay, people of both genders and all ages will benefit from the viewing of this show. All of television should be this good. The fact that this show has, for so long, been ignored by the Emmys is a travesty.

Mia: If only the Buffster could just find a boyfriend who doesn't need to drink platelets to survive. High point: Any time there's kissing. Low point: None.

Gilmore Girls
Lilly: Thoughtful portrayal of single mother struggling to raise teenage daughter in a small northeastern town.

Mia: Many, many, many, many, many, many cute boys. Plus it is nice to see single moms who sleep with their kid's teacher getting props instead of lectures from the Moral Majority.

Charmed
Lilly: While this show at least accurately portrays SOME typical Wiccan practices, the spells these girls routinely do are completely unrealistic. You cannot, for instance, travel through time or between dimensions without creating rifts in the space-time continuum. Were these girls really to transport themselves to seventeenth-century Puritan America, they would arrive there with their esophagi ripped

inside out, not neatly stuffed into a corset, as no one can travel through a wormhole and maintain their mass integrity. It is a simple matter of physics. Albert Einstein must be spinning in his grave.

Mia: Hello, witches in hot clothes. Like Sabrina, only better, because the boys are cuter, and sometimes they are in danger and the girls have to save them.

Thursday, January 22, G & T

Tina is so mad at Charlotte Brontë. She says *Jane Eyre* ruined her life.

She announced this at lunch. Right in front of Michael, who isn't supposed to know about the whole Jane Eyre technique of not-chasing-boys thing, but whatever. He admitted to never having read the book, so I think it is a safe bet he didn't know what Tina was talking about.

Still, it was way sad. Tina said she is giving up her romance novels. Giving them up because they led to the ruination of her relationship with Dave!

We were all very upset to hear about this. Tina *loves* reading romances. She reads about one a day.

But now she says that if it weren't for romance novels, she, and not Jasmine, would be going to the Rangers game with Dave Farouq El-Abar this Saturday.

And my pointing out that she doesn't even like hockey didn't seem to help.

Lilly and I both realized that this was a pivotal moment in Tina's adolescent growth. It needed to be pointed out to her that Dave, not Jane Eyre, was the one who'd pulled the plug on their relationship . . . and that, when looked at objectively, the whole thing was probably for the best. It was ludicrous for Tina to blame romance novels for her plight.

So Lilly and I very quickly drew up the following list, and presented it to Tina, in hopes that she would see the error of her ways:

MIA AND LILLY'S LIST OF ROMANTIC HEROINES AND THE VALUABLE LESSONS EACH TAUGHT US

1. Jane Eyre from *Jane Eyre*:
   Stick to your convictions and you will prevail.

2. Lorna Doone from *Lorna Doone*:
   Probably you are secretly royalty and an heiress, only no one has told you yet
   (this applies to Mia Thermopolis, as well).

3. Elizabeth Bennet from *Pride and Prejudice*:
   Boys like it when you are smart-alecky.

4. Scarlett O'Hara from *Gone With the Wind*:
   Ditto.

5. Maid Marian from *Robin Hood*:
   It is a good idea to learn how to use a bow and arrow.

6. Jo March from *Little Women*:
   Always keep a second copy of your manuscript

handy in case your vindictive little sister throws your first draft on the fire.

7. Anne Shirley from *Anne of Green Gables*:
   One word: Clairol.

8. Marguerite St. Just from *The Scarlet Pimpernel*:
   Check out your husband's rings before you marry him.

9. Catherine, from *Wuthering Heights*:
   Don't get too big for your britches or you, too, will have to wander the moors in lonely heartbreak after you die.

10. Tess from *Tess of the d'Urbervilles*:
    Ditto.

Tina, after reading the list, admitted tearfully that we were right, that romantic heroines from literature really were her friends, and that she could not, in good conscience, forsake them. We were all just breathing a sigh of relief (except for Michael and Boris—they were playing on Michael's GameBoy) when Shameeka made a sudden announcement, even more startling than Tina's:

"I'm trying out for cheerleading."

We were, of course, stunned. Not because

Shameeka would make a bad cheerleader—she is the most athletic of all of us, also the most attractive, and knows almost as much as Tina does about fashion and makeup.

It was just that, as Lilly so bluntly put it, "Why would you want to go and do something like *that*?"

"Because," Shameeka explained. "I am tired of letting Lana and her friends push me around. I am just as good as any of them. Why shouldn't I try out for the squad, even if I'm not in their little clique? I have just as good a chance of getting on the team as anybody else."

Lilly said, "While this is unarguably true, I feel I must warn you: Shameeka, if you try out for cheerleading, you might actually get on the squad. Are you prepared to subject yourself to the humiliation of cheering for Josh Richter as he chases after a ball?"

"Cheerleading has, for many years, suffered under the stigma of being inherently sexist," Shameeka said. "But I think the cheerleading community in general is making strides at asserting itself as a fast-growing sport for both men and women. It is a good way to keep fit and active, it combines two things I love dearly: dance and gymnastics, and will look excellent on my college applications. That is, of course, the only reason my father is allowing me to try out. That and the fact that George W. Bush was a cheerleader. And that I won't be allowed to attend any post-game parties."

I didn't doubt this last part. Mr. Taylor, Shameeka's dad, was way strict.

But as for the rest of it, well, I wasn't sure. Plus, her speech sounded a little planned and, well, defensive.

"Does that mean that if you get on the squad," I wanted to know, "you'll stop eating lunch with us, and go sit over there?"

I pointed at the long table across the caf from ours, at which Lana and Josh and all of their school-spirit-minded, incredibly well coifed cronies sat. The thought of losing Shameeka, who was always so elegant and yet at the same time sensible, to the Dark Side made my heart ache.

"Of course not," Shameeka said disparagingly. "Getting on the Albert Einstein High School cheerleading squad is not going to change my friendships with all of you one iota. I will still be the camera person for your television show—" She nodded to Lilly "—and your Bio partner—" to me "—and your lipstick consultant—" to Tina "—and your portrait model—" to Ling Su. "I just may not be around as much, if I get on the squad."

We all sat there, reflecting upon this great change that might befall us. If Shameeka made the squad, it would, of course, strike a blow for geeky girls everywhere. But it would also necessarily rob us of Shameeka, who would be forced to spend all of her free time practicing doing the splits and taking the bus to Westchester for away games with Rye Country Day.

But there was even more to it than that. If Shameeka made the cheerleading squad, it would mean she is good at something—REALLY REALLY good at something, not just a little good at everything, which we already knew about her. If Shameeka turned out to be REALLY REALLY good at something, then I would be the ONLY one at our lunch table without a recognizable talent.

And I swear it wasn't for this reason alone that I was hoping so fervently that Shameeka wouldn't make the team. I mean, I seriously wanted her to make it, if that was really what she wanted.

Only . . . only I REALLY don't want to be the only one who doesn't have a talent!!!! I REALLY REALLY don't!!!!!!!

The silence at the table was palpable . . . well, except for the *bing-bing-bing* of Michael's electronic game. Boys—apparently even perfect boys, like Michael—are immune to things like mood.

But I can tell you, the mood of this year so far has been pretty bad. In fact, if things don't start looking up soon, I may have to write this entire year off as a do-over.

Still no clue as to what my secret talent might be. One thing I'm pretty sure it's *not* is psychology. It was hard work talking Tina out of giving up her books! And we didn't manage to convince Shameeka not to try out for cheerleading. I guess I can see why she'd want to do it—I mean, it might be a *little* fun.

Though why anyone would willingly want to spend that much time with Lana Weinberger is beyond me.

Thursday, January 22, French

Mademoiselle Klein is *not* happy with Tina and me for skipping yesterday.

Of course I told her we didn't skip, that we had a medical emergency that necessitated a trip to Ho's for Tampax, but I am not sure Mademoiselle Klein believed me. You would think she would show some feminine solidarity with the whole surfing the crimson-wave thing, but apparently not. At least she didn't write us up. She let us off with a warning and assigned us a five-hundred-word essay each (in French, of course) about the Maginot Line.

But that isn't even what I want to write about. What I want to write about is this:

MY DAD RULES!!!!!

And not just a country, either. He totally got me out of the Contessa's black-and-white ball!!!!

What happened was—at least according to Mr. G, who just caught me outside in the hall and filled me in—the filibuster over the parking meters was finally broken (after thirty-six hours) and my mom was finally able to get through to my dad (those in favor of charging for parking meters won. It is a victory for the environment as well as for me. But I cannot feel fully vindicated for the post-introduction-speech-to-my-people mocking I endured at Grandmère's hands, due to the fact that the true winner in all of this is the Genovian infrastructure).

Anyway, my dad fully said that I did not have to go to the Contessa's party. Not only that, but he said he had never heard anything so ridiculous in his life, that the only feud going on between our family and the royal family of Monaco is Grandmère's. Apparently she and the Contessa have been in competition since finishing school, and Grandmère had just wanted to show off her granddaughter, about whom books have been written and movies have been made. Apparently the Contessa's only granddaughter will also be at the ball, but she's never had a movie based on her life, and in fact is kind of like a sadsack who got kicked out of finishing school for never learning how to ski right, or something.

So I am free! Free to spend tomorrow night with my only love! I cat-on-the-roofed Michael for nothing! Everything is going to be all right, despite my lack of lucky underwear. I can feel it in my bones.

I am so happy, I feel like writing a poem. I will shield it from Tina, however, because it is unseemly to gloat over one's own fortunes when the fortunes of another are so exceedingly wretched (Tina found out who Jasmine is: a girl who goes to Trinity, with Dave. Her father is an oil sheik, too. Jasmine has aquamarine braces and her screenname is IluvJustin2345).

HOMEWORK

Algebra: probs at end of Chapt. 11

English: in journal, describe feelings pertaining to reading John Donne's *The Bait*

Bio: don't know, Shameeka is doing it for me

Health and Safety: Chapter 2, Environmental Hazards and You

G & T: figure out secret talent

French: Chapitre Onze, écrivez une narratif, 300 words, double spaced, plus 500 wds on snails

World Civ: 500 words, describe origins of Armenian conflict

Poem for Michael

Oh, Michael,
soon we'll be parkin'
in front of Grand Moff Tarkin
Enjoying veggie moo shu
to the beeps of R2-D2
And maybe even holding hands
while gazing upon the Tatooine sands
And knowing that our love by far
has more fire power than the Death Star
And though they may blow up our planet
and kill every creature living on it
Like Leia and Han, in the stars above,
they can never destroy our love—
Like the Millennium Falcon in hyperdrive
our love will continue to thrive and thrive.

Thursday, January 22, limo on way home from Grandmère's

It takes a big person to admit she's wrong—Grandmère is the one who taught me that.

And if it's true, then I must be even bigger than my five feet nine inches. Because I've been wrong. I've been wrong about Grandmère. All this time, when I thought she was inhuman and perhaps even sent down from an alien mothership to observe life on this planet and then report back to her superiors? Yeah, turns out Grandmère really is human, just like me.

How did I find this out? How did I discover that the dowager princess of Genovia did not, after all, sell her soul to the Prince of Darkness as I have often surmised?

I learned it today when I walked into Grandmère's suite at the Plaza, fully prepared to do battle with her over the whole Contessa Trevanni thing. I was going to be all, "Grandmère, Dad says I don't have to go, and guess what, I'm not going to."

That's what I was going to say, anyway.

Except that when I walked in and saw her, the words practically died on my lips. Because Grandmère looked as if someone had run over her with a truck! Seriously. She was sitting there in the dark—she had had these purple scarves thrown over the lampshades because she said the light was hurting her eyes—and she wasn't even dressed properly. She had on a velvet lounging robe and some slippers and had a cashmere throw blanket covering her lap and that was it, and her hair was all in curlers and if her eyeliner hadn't been tattooed on, I swear it would have been all smeared. She wasn't even enjoying a Sidecar, her favorite refreshment, or anything. She was just sitting there, with Rommel trembling on her lap, looking like death warmed over. Grandmère, not the dog.

"Grandmère," I couldn't help crying out, when I saw her. "Are you all right? Are you sick or something?"

But all Grandmère said was, in a voice so unlike her own normally quite strident one that I could barely believe it belonged to the same woman, "No, I'm fine. At least I will be. Once I get over the humiliation."

"Humiliation? What humiliation?" I went over to kneel by her chair. "Grandmère, are you sure you aren't sick? You aren't even smoking!"

"I'll be all right," she said, weakly. "It will be weeks before I'll be able to show my face in public. But I'm a Renaldo. I'm strong. I will recover."

Actually Grandmère is technically only a Renaldo by marriage, but at that point I wasn't going to argue with her, because I thought there was something genuinely wrong, like her uterus had fallen out in the shower or something (this happened to one of the women in the condo community down in Boca where

Lilly and Michael's grandmother lives. Also it happens a lot to the cows in *All Creatures Great and Small*).

"Grandmère," I said, kind of looking around, in case her uterus was lying on the floor somewhere or whatever. "Do you want me to call a doctor?"

"No doctor can cure what is wrong with me," Grandmère assured me. "I am only suffering from the mortification of having a granddaughter who doesn't love me."

I had no idea what she was talking about. Sure, I don't like Grandmère so much sometimes. Sometimes I even think I hate her. But I don't not love her. I guess. At least I've never said so, to her face.

"Grandmère, what are you talking about? Of course I love you—"

"Then why won't you come with me to the Contessa Trevanni's black-and-white ball?" Grandmère wailed.

Blinking rapidly, I could only stammer, "Wh-what?"

"Your father says you will not go to the ball," Grandmère said. "He says you have no wish to go!"

"Grandmère," I said. "You know I don't want to go. You know that Michael and I—"

"*That boy!*" Grandmère cried. "*That boy* again!"

"Grandmère, stop calling him that," I said. "You know his name perfectly well."

"And I suppose this Michael—" Grandmère sniffed "—is more important to you than *I* am. I suppose you consider *his* feelings over mine in this case."

The answer to that, of course, was a resounding *yes*. But I didn't want to be rude. I said, "Grandmère, tomorrow night is our first date. Mine and Michael's, I mean. It's really important to me."

"And I suppose the fact that it was really important to *me* that you attend this ball—that is of no consequence?" Grandmère actually looked, for a moment, as she sat gazing down at me so miserably, like she had tears in her eyes. But maybe it was only a trick of the not very clear light. "The fact that Elena Trevanni has been, since I was a little girl, always lording it over me, because she was born into a more respected and aristocratic family than I was? That until I married your grandfather, she always had nicer clothes and shoes and handbags than my parents could afford for me? That she still thinks she is so much better than me, because she married a *compt* who had no responsibilities or property, just unlimited wealth, whereas I have been forced to work my fingers to the bone in order to make Genovia the vacation paradise it is today? And that I was hoping that just this once, by revealing what a lovely and accomplished granddaughter I have, I could show her up?"

I was stunned. I'd had no idea why this stupid ball was so important to her. I thought it had just been because she'd wanted to try to split Michael and me up, or get me to start liking Prince René instead, so that the two of us could unite our families in holy matrimony someday and create a race of super-royals. It had never occurred to me that there might be some underlying, mitigating circumstance . . .

Such as that the Contessa Trevanni, was, in essence, Grandmère's Lana Weinberger.

Because that's what it sounded like. Like Elena Trevanni had tortured and teased Grandmère as mercilessly as I had been tortured and teased by Lana through the years.

I wondered if Elena, like Lana, had ever suggested to Grandmère that she wear Band-Aids on her boobs instead of a bra. If she had said this to Clarisse Renaldo, she was a far, far braver soul than I.

"And now," Grandmère said, very sadly, "I have to tell her that my granddaughter doesn't love me enough to put aside her new boyfriend for one single night."

I realized, with a sinking heart, what I had to do. I mean, I knew how Grandmère felt. If there had been some way—any way at all—that I could have shown up Lana—you know, besides going out with her boyfriend, which I had already done, but that had ended up humiliating *me* way more than it had Lana—I'd have done it. Anything.

Because when someone is as mean and cruel and just downright nasty as Lana is—not just to me, either, but to all the girls at Albert Einstein High who weren't blessed with good looks and school spirit—she fully deserves to have her nose rubbed in it.

It was so weird to think about someone like Grandmère, who seemed so incredibly sure of herself, having a Lana Weinberger in her life. I mean, I had always pictured Grandmère being the type of person who, if Lana flipped her long blonde hair onto her desk, would go all Crouching Tiger on her and deliver a Ferragamo to the face.

But maybe there was someone even Grandmère was a little bit afraid of. And maybe that person was Contessa Trevanni.

And while it is not true that I love Grandmère more than I love Michael—I do not love anyone more than I love Michael, except of course for Fat Louie—I did feel sorrier for Grandmère at that moment than I did for myself. You know, if Michael ended up dumping me because I canceled our date. It sounds incredible, but it's true.

So I went, even as I said them not quite believing the words were coming out of my mouth, "All right, Grandmère, I'll put in an appearance at your ball."

A miraculous change overcame Grandmère. She seemed to brighten right up.

"Really, Amelia?" she asked, reaching out to grasp one of my hands. "Will you really do this for me?"

I was, I knew, going to lose Michael forever. But like my mother had said, if he didn't understand, then he probably hadn't been right for me in the first place.

I am such a pushover. But she just looked so happy.

She flung off the cashmere throw—and Rommel—and rang for her maid to bring her a Sidecar and her cigarettes, and then we moved on to the day's lesson—how to ask for the number of the nearest taxi company in five different languages.

All I want to know is: What.

Not about why I would ever need to call a taxi in Hindustani.

I mean what—WHAT????—am I going to tell Michael? I mean, seriously. If he doesn't dump me now then there's something wrong with him. And since I know there is nothing wrong with him, I know that I am about to be dumped.

For which all I can say is THERE IS NO JUSTICE IN THE WORLD. NONE.

Since Lilly has her breakfast meeting with the producers of the made-for-TV movie of my life tomorrow morning, I guess I will break the news to Michael then. That way he can dump me in time for Homeroom. Maybe then I will have stopped crying before Lana sees me in Algebra first period. I don't think I'll be able to take her mockery, after already having my heart ripped from my body and flung across the floor.

I hate myself.

Thursday, January 22, the loft

I saw the movie of my life. My mom taped it for me while I was in Genovia. She thought Mr. G recorded a Jets game over it, but it turned out he hadn't.

The guy who played Michael was a total babe. In the movie, he and I end up together in the end.

Too bad that in real life, he is going to dump me tomorrow . . . even though Tina doesn't think so.

This is very nice of her and everything, but the fact is, he is totally going to. I mean, it really is a matter of pride. If a girl with whom you have been going out for a full thirty-four days cancels your very first date, you really have no choice but to break up with her. I mean, I totally understand. *I* would break up with me. It is clear now that royal teens can't be like normal ones. I mean, for people like me and Prince William, duty will always have to come first. Who is going to be able to understand that, let alone put up with it?

Tina says Michael can, and will. Tina says Michael won't break up with me because he loves me. I said yes he will, because he only loves me as a friend.

"Clearly Michael loves you as more than just a friend," Tina keeps saying into the phone. "I mean, you guys kissed!"

"Yes," I say. "But Kenny and I kissed, and I did not like him as more than just a friend."

"This is a completely different situation," Tina says.

"How?"

"Because you and Michael are meant to be together!" Tina sounds exasperated. "Your star chart says so! You and Kenny were never meant for one another, he is a Cancer."

Tina's astrological predictions notwithstanding, there is no evidence that Michael feels more strongly for me than he does for, say, Judith Gershner. Yes, he wrote me that poem that mentioned the L word. But that was an entire month ago, during which period I was in another country. He has not renewed any such protestations since my return. I think it highly likely that tomorrow will be the straw that broke the hot guy's back. I mean, why would Michael waste his time on a girl like me, who can't even stand up to her own grandmother? I'm sure if Michael's grandmother had been all, "Michael, you've got to go to Bingo with me Friday night, because Olga Krakowski, my childhood rival, will be there, and I want to show you off," he'd have been all, "Sorry, Gram, no can do."

No, I'm the spineless one.

And I'm the one who now must suffer for it.

I wonder if it is too late in the school year to transfer. Because I really don't think I can take going to the same school as Michael after we are broken up. Seeing him in the hallway between classes, at lunch, and in G and T, knowing he was once mine, but that I'd lost him, might just kill me.

But is there another school in Manhattan that might take a talentless, spineless reject like me? Doubtful.

For Michael

Oh, Michael, my one true love
We had all new pleasures yet to prove
But I lost you due to my lack of spine
And now through the years, for you I will pine.

Well. That's it. I told him.

He hasn't dumped me. Yet. In fact, he was way nice about the whole thing.

"No, really, Mia," was what he said. "I understand. You're a princess. Duty comes first."

Maybe he just didn't want to dump me at school, in front of everyone?

I told him that I would try to get out of the ball early if I could. He said that if I did, I should stop by. The Moscovitzes' apartment, I mean.

I know what this means, of course:

That he is going to dump me there.

OH, MY GOD, WHAT IS WRONG WITH ME????? I have known Michael for years and years. He is NOT the type of boy who would dump a girl just because she has a family obligation that must take precedence over a date with him. HE IS NOT LIKE THAT. THAT IS WHY I LOVE HIM.

But why can't I stop thinking that the only reason he didn't dump me right then and there is because he couldn't do it in my own limo, in front of my bodyguard and driver? I mean, for all Michael knew, Lars might be trained to beat up boys who try to dump me in front of him.

I HAVE GOT TO STOP THIS. MICHAEL IS NOT DAVE FAROUQ EL-ABAR. He is NOT going to dump me because of this.

Except why do I feel like I know now how Jane Eyre must have felt when she learned the truth about Bertha on her wedding day? No, Michael doesn't have a wife, that I know of. But it's entirely possible that my relationship with him, like Jane's with Mr. Rochester, is coming to an end. And I can think of no earthly way it can ever be repaired. I mean, it's possible that tonight, when I go by the Moscovitzes' place, it will be in flames, and I will be able to prove myself worthy of Michael's love by selflessly saving his mother, or perhaps his dog, Pavlov, from the fire.

But other than that, I don't see us getting back together. I will of course give him his birthday present, because I went to all the trouble of stealing it.

But I know it won't do any good.

What is WRONG with me???? This better be PMS. Because if this is what love is like all the time, I don't want to be in love anymore!!!!!!!!!!!!!!!!!!!!!!!!!!!!

Friday, January 23, still Homeroom

They just announced the name of the newest member of the Albert Einstein High junior varsity cheerleading squad. It is Shameeka Taylor.

Great. Just great. So that's it. I am now officially the only person I know who has absolutely no discernible talent.

I am a reject in *every* way.

Friday, January 23, Algebra

Michael did not stop by here between classes. It is the first day all week that he hasn't slipped in to say hi on his way to AP English, three classrooms away from this one.

I am totally trying not to take it personally, but there is this little voice inside of me going, *That's it! It's over! He's dumping you!*

I'm sure Kate Bosworth doesn't have a voice like this that lives inside her. WHY couldn't I have been born Kate Bosworth instead of me, Mia Thermopolis?

To make matters worse—as if I can even care about something so trivial—Lana just turned around to hiss, "Don't think just because your little friend made the squad that anything is going to change between us, Mia. She's as much of a pathetic geekette as you are. They only let her on the squad to fill our freak quota."

Then she whipped her head around again—but not as fast as she should have. Because a lot of her hair was still draped across my desk.

And when I slammed my Algebra I–II text closed as hard as I could—which is what I did next—a lot of her silky, awapuhi-scented locks got trapped between pages 210 and 211.

Lana shrieked in pain. Mr. G, up at the chalkboard, turned around, saw where the screaming was coming from, and sighed.

"Mia," he said, tiredly. "Lana. What now?"

Lana stabbed an index finger in my direction. "She slammed her book on my hair!"

I shrugged innocently. "I didn't know her hair was in my book. Why can't she keep her hair to herself, anyway?"

Mr. Gianini looked bored. "Lana," he said. "If you can't keep your hair under control, I recommend braids. Mia, don't slam your book. It should be open to page two eleven, where I want you to read from Section Two. Out loud."

I read out loud from Section Two, but not without a certain primness. For once, vengeance on Lana had been mine, and I had NOT been sent to the principal's office. Oh, it was sweet. Sweet, sweet vindication.

Although I don't even know why I have to learn this stuff, it isn't as if the Palais de Genovia isn't full of dweeby staffers who are just dying to multiply fractions for me.

Polynomials
term: variable(s) multiplied by a coefficient

monomial: Polynomial w/ one term
binomial: Polynomial w/ two terms
trinomial: Polynomial w/ three terms

Degree of polynomial = the degree of the term with the highest degree

In my delight over the pain I had brought upon my enemy, I almost forgot about the fact that my heart is broken. Must keep in mind that Michael is dumping me after the black-and-white ball tonight. Why can't I FOCUS???? Must be love. I am sick with it.

Friday, January 23, Health and Safety

Why do you look like you just ate a sock?

I don't. How was your breakfast meeting?

You do, too. The meeting went GREAT.

Really? Did they agree to print a full-page letter of apology in *Variety?*

No, better. Did something happen between you and my brother? Because I saw him looking all furtive in the hallway just now.

FURTIVE? Furtive like how? Like he was looking for Judith Gershner to ask her out tonight????

No, more like he was looking for a pay phone. Why would he ask out Judith Gershner? How many times do I have to tell you, he likes you, not J.G.

He used to like me, you mean. Before I was forced to cancel our date tonight due to Grandmère forcing me to go to a ball.

A ball? Really. Ugh. But excuse me. Michael isn't going to ask some other girl to go out with him tonight just because you can't make it. I mean, he was really looking forward to going with you. Not just for concupiscent reasons, either.

REALLY????

Yes, you loser. What did you think? I mean, you guys are going out.

But that's just it. We haven't. Gone out yet, I mean.

So? You'll go out sometime when you don't have a ball to go to instead.

You don't think he's going to dump me?

Uh, not unless something heavy fell on his head between now and the last time I saw him. Guys with cranial damage can't generally be held responsible for their actions.

Why would something heavy fall on his head?

I'm being facetious. Do you want to hear about my meeting, or not?

Yes. What happened?

They told me they want to option my show.

What does that mean?

It means that they will take Lilly Tells It Like It Is *around to the networks to see if anybody wants to buy it. To be a real show. On a real channel. Not like public access. Like ABC or Lifetime or VH1 or something.*

Lilly!!!! THAT IS SO GREAT!!!!

Yes, I know. Oops, gotta go. Wheeton's looking this way.

Note to self: Look up words *concupiscent* and *facetious.*

Friday, January 23, G & T

Lunch was just one big celebration today. Everyone had something to be happy about:

- Shameeka, for making the cheerleading squad and striking a blow for tall geeky girls everywhere (even though of course Shameeka looks like a supermodel and can wrap both her ankles around her head, but whatever).
- Lilly, for getting her TV show optioned.
- Tina, for finally deciding to give up on Dave but not on romance in general and get on with her life.
- Ling Su for getting her drawing of Joe, the stone lion, into the school art fair.
- And Boris for just, well, being Boris. Boris is always happy.

You will notice that I did not mention Michael. That is because I do not know what Michael's mental state at lunch was, whether or not he was happy or sad or concupiscent or whatever. That is because Michael didn't show up to lunch. He said, when he breezed by my locker just before fourth period, "Hey, I've got some things to do, I'll see you in G and T, okay?"

Some things to do.

I should, of course, just ask him. I should just be

like, "Look, are you going to break up with me over this, or what?" Because I would really like to know, one way or the other.

Except that I can't just go up and ask Michael what the deal is between us, because right now he is busy with Boris, going over band stuff. Michael's band is comprised of (so far) Michael (precision bass), Boris (electric violin), that tall guy Paul from the Computer Club (keyboards), this guy from the AEHS marching band called Trevor (guitar), and Felix, this scary-looking twelfth grader with a goatee that's bushier than Mr. Gianini's (drums). They still don't have a name for the band, or a place to practice. But they seem to think that Mr. Kreblutz, the head custodian, will let them into the band practice rooms on weekends if they can get him tickets to the Westminster Kennel Show next month. Mr. Kreblutz is a huge bichon-frise fan.

The fact that Michael can concentrate on all this band stuff while our relationship is falling apart is just further proof that he is a true musician, completely dedicated to his art. I, being the talentless freak that I am, can of course think of nothing *but* my heartbreak. Michael's ability to remain focused in spite of any personal pain he might be suffering is evidence of his genius.

Either that or he never cared that much about me in the first place.

I prefer to believe the former.

Oh, that I had some kind of outlet, such as music, into which to pour the suffering I am currently feeling! But alas, I'm no artist. I just have to sit here in silent pain, while around me, more gifted souls express their innermost angst through song, dance, and filmography.

Well, okay, just through filmography since there are no singers or dancers in fifth-period G and T. Instead we just have Lilly, putting together what she is calling her quintessential episode of *Lilly Tells It Like It Is*, a show that will explore the seamy underbelly of that American institution known as Starbucks. It is Lilly's contention that Starbucks, through the introduction of the Starbucks card (with which caffeine addicts can pay for their fix electronically) is actually a secret branch of the Central Intelligence Agency that is tracing the movements of America's intelligentsia—writers, editors, and other known liberal agitators—through their coffee consumption.

Whatever. I don't even like coffee.

Aw, crud. The bell.

HOMEWORK

Algebra: Who cares?

English: Everything sucks.

Bio: I hate life.

Health and Safety: Mr. Wheeton is in love, too. I should warn him to get out now, while he still can.

G & T: I shouldn't even be in this class.

French: Why does this language even exist? Everyone there speaks English anyway.

World Civ: What does it matter? We're all just going to die.

Friday, January 23, 6 p.m.,
Grandmère's suite at the Plaza

Grandmère made me come here straight after school so that Paolo could start getting us ready for the ball. I didn't know Paolo makes house calls, but apparently he does. Only for royalty, he assured me, and, of course, Madonna.

I explained to him about how I am growing out my hair on account of boys liking long hair better than short hair, and Paolo made some tut-tutting noises, but he slapped some curlers into it to try to get rid of the triangular shape, and I guess it worked, because my hair looks pretty good. All of me looks pretty good. On the outside, anyway.

Too bad that inside, I'm completely busted.

I am trying not to show it, though. You know, because I want Grandmère to think I am having a good time. I mean, I am only doing this for her. Because she is an old lady and my grandmother and she campaigned against the Nazis and all of that, for which someone has to give her some props.

I just hope someday she appreciates it. My supreme sacrifice, I mean. But I doubt she ever will. Seventy-something-year-old ladies—particularly dowager princesses—never seem to remember what it was like to be fourteen and in love.

Well, I guess it is time to go. Grandmère has on this

slinky black number with glitter all over it. She looks like Diana Ross. Only with no eyebrows. And old. And white.

She says I look like a snowdrop. Hmmm, just what I always wanted, to look like a snowdrop.

Maybe that's my secret talent. I have the amazing ability to resemble a snowdrop.

My parents must be so proud.

Yep. In the bathroom. In the bathroom once again,
where I always seem to end up at dances. Why is that?

The Contessa's bathroom is a little bit overdone. It
is nice and everything, but I don't know if I'd have
chosen flaming wall sconces as part of my bathroom
decor. I mean, even at the palace, we don't have any
flaming wall sconces. Although it looks very romantic
and *Ivanhoe*-y and all, it is actually a pretty serious fire
hazard, besides being probably a health risk, considering the carcinogens they must be giving off.

But whatever. That isn't even the real question—
why anyone would have flaming wall sconces in the
bathroom. The real question, of course, is this: if I am
supposedly descended from all these strong women—
you know, Rosagunde, who strangled that warlord with
her braid, and Agnes, who jumped off that bridge, not
to mention Grandmère, who allegedly kept the Nazis
from trashing Genovia by having Hitler and Mussolini
over for tea—why is it that I am such a pushover?

I mean, seriously. I totally fell for Grandmère's
whole riff about wanting to show up Elena Trevanni
with her pretty and accomplished—yeah, and looking
like a snowdrop—granddaughter. I actually felt sorry
for her. I had empathy for Grandmère, not realizing
then—as I do now—that Grandmère is completely

devoid of human emotion, and that the whole thing was just a charade to trick me into coming so she could parade me around as PRINCE RENÉ'S NEW GIRL-FRIEND!!!!!!!!!!!!!!!!

To his credit, René seems to have known nothing about it. He looked as surprised as I was when Grandmère presented me to her supposed archrival, who, thanks to the skill of her plastic surgeon, looks about thirty years younger than Grandmère, though they are supposedly the same age.

But I think the Contessa maybe went a little far with the surgery thing—it is so hard to know when to say when. I mean, look at poor Michael Jackson—because she really does, just like Grandmère said, resemble a walleyed bass a little bit. Like her eyes are sort of far apart on account of the skin around them being stretched so tight.

When Grandmère introduced me—"Contessa, may I present to you my granddaughter, Princess Amelia Mignonette Grimaldi Renaldo" (she always leaves out the Thermopolis)—I thought everything was going to be all right. Well, not everything, of course, since directly after the ball, I knew I was going to go over to my best friend's house and maybe–possibly–probably get dumped by her brother. But you know, everything at the ball.

But then Grandmère added, "And of course you know Amelia's beau, Prince Pierre René Grimaldi Alberto."

Beau? BEAU??? René and I exchanged quick glances. It was only then that I noticed that, standing right next to the Contessa, was a girl who had to have been her own granddaughter, the one who'd been kicked out of finishing school. She was kind of plain and sad-looking, though her slinky black dress was exactly the kind I'd have wanted to wear to the Prom—were I ever asked. Still, she wasn't exactly wearing it with confidence.

So while I was standing there getting totally red in the face, and probably not resembling a snowdrop as much as a candy cane, the Contessa cocked her head so she could look at me and went, "So that rascal René has finally been snatched up, and by *your* granddaughter, Clarisse. How satisfying that must be for you."

Then the Contessa shot her own granddaughter—whom she introduced to me as Bella—a look of pure malevolence that caused Bella to cringe.

And I realized all at once what, exactly, was going on.

Then Grandmère said, "Isn't it, though, Elena?" And then to René and me she went, "Come along, children," and we followed her, René looking amused, but me? I was *seething*!

"I can't believe you did that," I cried, as soon as we were out of the Contessa's earshot.

"Did what, Amelia?" Grandmère asked, nodding to some guy in traditional African garb.

"Told that woman that René and I are going out,"

I said, "when we most certainly are not. I know you only did it to make me look better than poor Bella."

"René," Grandmère said, sweetly. She can be very sweet when she wants to be. "Be an angel and see if you can find us some champagne, would you?"

René, still looking cynically amused—the way Enrique always looks in Doritos commercials—moved off in search of libation.

"Really, Amelia," Grandmère said, when he was gone. "Must you be so rude to poor René? I am only trying to make your cousin feel welcome and at home."

"There is a difference," I said, "between making my cousin feel welcome and wanted, and trying to pass him off as my boyfriend!"

"Well, what's so wrong with René, anyway?" Grandmère wanted to know. All around us, elegant people in tuxedos and evening gowns were heading to the dance floor, where a full orchestra was playing that song Audrey Hepburn sang in that movie about Tiffany's. Everyone was dressed in either black or white or both. The Contessa's ballroom bore a significant resemblance to the penguin enclosure at the Central Park Zoo, where I had once sobbed my eyes out after discovering the truth about my heritage.

"He's extremely charming," Grandmère went on, "and quite cosmopolitan. Not to mention devilishly handsome. How can you possibly prefer a high school boy to a *prince*?"

"Because, Grandmère," I said. "I love him."

"Love," Grandmère said, looking toward the big glass ceiling overhead. *"Pfuit!"*

"Yes, Grandmère," I said. "I do. The way you loved Grandpère—and don't try to deny it, because I know you did. Now you've got to stop harboring a secret desire to make Prince René your grandson-in-law, because it is not going to happen."

Grandmère looked blandly innocent. "I don't know what you can mean," she said, with a sniff.

"Cut it out, Grandmère. You want me to go out with Prince René, for no other reason than that he is a royal, and it will make the Contessa feel bad. Well, it isn't going to happen. Even if Michael and I were to break up—" which might possibly happen sooner than she thought "—I wouldn't get together with *René!*"

Grandmère finally began to look as if she might believe me. "Fine," she said, without much grace. "I will stop calling René your beau. But you must dance with him. At least once."

"Grandmère." The last thing in the world I felt like was dancing. "Please. Not tonight. You don't know—"

"Amelia," Grandmère said, in a different tone of voice than she'd used thus far. "One dance. That is all I am asking for. I believe you owe it to me."

"*I* owe it to *you?*" I couldn't help bursting out laughing at that one. "How so?"

"Oh, only because of a little something," Grandmère

said, all innocently, "that was recently found to be missing from the palace museum."

All of my Renaldo fighting spirit went right out the Contessa's French doors to her backyard patio when I heard this. I felt as if someone had punched me in my snowdrop stomach. Had Grandmère really said what I *thought* she'd said???

Swallowing hard, I went, "Wh-what?"

"Yes." Grandmère looked at me meaningfully. "A priceless object—only one out of a group of several, almost identical items—that were given to me by my very dear friend, Mr. Richard Nixon, the deceased former American president, has been found to be missing. I realize the person who took it thought it would never be missed, because it wasn't the only such item, and they all did look much alike. Still, it held great sentimental value for me. Dick was such a dear, sweet friend to Genovia while he was in office, for all his later troubles. *But you wouldn't happen to know anything about any of this, would you, Amelia?*"

She had me! She had me, and she knew it. I don't know how she knew—undoubtedly through the black arts, in which I suspect Grandmère of being well versed—but clearly, she knew. I was dead. I was so, so dead. I don't know if, being a member of the royal family and all, I was above the law back in Genovia, but I for one did not want to find out.

I should, I realize now, merely have dissembled. I

should have been all, "Priceless object? What priceless object?"

But I knew it was no good to lie. My nostrils would give me away. Instead, I went, in this squeaky, high-pitched voice I barely recognized as my own, "You know what, Grandmère? I'll be happy to dance with René. No problem!"

Grandmère looked extremely satisfied. She said, "Yes, I thought you would feel that way." Then her drawn-on eyebrows went up. "Oh, look, here comes Prince René with our drinks. Sweet of him, don't you think?"

Anyway, that's how it happened that I was forced to dance with Prince René—who is a good dancer, but whatever, he's no Michael. I mean, he's never even seen *Buffy the Vampire Slayer* and he thinks Windows is pretty swell.

While we were dancing, though, this incredible thing happened. René went, "Could you believe that Bella Trevanni? Look at her, over there. She looks like a plant someone forgot to water."

I glanced around to see what he was talking about, and sure enough, there was poor sad Bella, dancing with some old guy who must have been a friend of her grandmother's. She looked extremely pained, like the old guy was talking to her about his investment portfolio or something. Then again, with someone like the Contessa for a grandmother, maybe pained was an expression Bella wore all the time. And my heart swelled with sympathy for her, because I so know what it is like to be somewhere you don't want to be, dancing with someone you don't like. . . .

I looked up at René and said, "When this dance is over, ask her for the next one."

It was René's turn to look pained. "Must I?"

"Come on, René," I said, severely. "Ask her to dance. It will be the thrill of her life to be asked to dance by a handsome prince."

"But not so much for you, eh?" René said, still wearing his cynical smile.

"René," I said. "No offense. But I already met my prince, long before I ever met you. The only problem is, if I don't get out of here soon, I don't know how much longer he's going to be my prince, because I already missed the movie we were supposed to see together, and pretty soon it's going to be too late even for me to stop by—"

"Never fear, Your Highness," René said, twirling me around. "If fleeing the ball is your desire, I will see to it that your wish is fulfilled."

I looked at him kind of dubiously. I mean, why was René being so nice to me all of a sudden? Maybe for the same reason I wanted him to dance with Bella? Because he felt sorry for me?

"Um," I said. "Okay."

And that's how I ended up in this bathroom. René

told me to hide, and that he'd get Lars to flag down a cab, and once he'd gotten one, and the coast was clear, René would knock three times, signaling that Grandmère was too otherwise occupied to notice my defection. Then, René promised, he'd tell her I must have eaten a bad truffle, since I'd looked queasy, and Lars had taken me home.

It doesn't matter, of course. Any of this, I mean. Because I am just going to end up at Michael's in time for him to dump me. Maybe he'll feel bad about it, you know, after I give him his birthday present. Then again, maybe he'll just be glad to be rid of me. Who knows? I've given up trying to figure out men. They are a breed apart.

Oops, there's René's knock. Gotta go.

To meet my fate.

Now I know how Jane Eyre must have felt when she returned to Thornfield Hall to find it all burned to the ground and everyone telling her everybody inside of it was killed in the fire.

Only then she finds out Mr. Rochester didn't die, and Jane's, like, super happy, because, you know, in spite of what he tried to do to her, she loves him.

That's how I feel right now. Super happy. Because I fully don't think Michael is going to break up with me after all!!!!

Not that I ever thought he was going to . . . well, not REALLY. Because he is NOT that kind of guy. But I was really, really scared he might when I was standing outside the Moscovitzes' apartment, you know, with my finger on the buzzer. I was standing there going, *Why am I even doing this? I am fully just walking into heartbreak. I should turn around and have Lars flag down another cab and just go back to the loft.* I hadn't even bothered changing out of my stupid ball gown, because what was the point? I was just going to be on my way home in a few minutes anyway, and I could change there.

So I'm standing there in the hallway, and Lars is behind me going on about his stupid boar hunt in Belize, because that is all he talks about anymore, and I hear Pavlov, Michael's dog, barking because someone is at the door, and I'm going, inside my head, *Okay, when he breaks up with me, I am NOT going to cry. I am going to remember Rosagunde and Agnes, and I am going to be strong like they were strong. . . .*

And then Michael opened the door. He looked kind of taken aback by my apparel, I could tell. I thought maybe it was because he hadn't counted on having to break up with a snowdrop. But there was nothing I could do about that, though I did remember at the last minute that I was still wearing my tiara, which I suppose might intimidate, you know, some boys.

So I took it off and went, "Well, I'm here," which is a toolish thing to say, because, well, duh, I was standing there, wasn't I?

But Michael kind of seemed to recover himself. He went, "Oh, hey, come in, you look . . . you look really beautiful," which of course is exactly the kind of thing a guy who is about to break up with you would say, you know to kind of bolster your ego before he grinds it beneath his heel.

But whatever, I went in, and so did Lars, and Michael went, "Lars, my mom and dad are in the living room watching *Dateline*, if you want to join them," which Lars totally did, because you could tell he didn't want to hang around and listen to the Big Breakup.

So then Michael and I were alone in the foyer. I was twirling my tiara around in my hands, trying to think of what to say. I'd been trying to think what to say the whole way down in the cab, but I hadn't been very successful.

Then Michael went, "Well, did you eat yet? Because I've got some veggie burgers. . . ."

I looked up from the parquet floor tiles, which I had been examining very closely, since it was easier than looking into Michael's peat-bog eyes, which always suck me in until I feel like I can't move anymore. They used to punish criminals in ancient Celtic societies by making them walk into a peat bog. If they sank, you know, they were guilty, and if not, they were innocent. Only you always sink when you walk into a peat bog. They uncovered a bunch of bodies from one in Ireland not too long ago, and they, like, still had all their teeth and hair and stuff. They were totally preserved. It was way gross.

That's how I feel when I look into Michael's eyes. Not preserved and gross, but like I'm trapped in a peat bog. Only I don't mind, because it's warm and nice and cozy in there. . . .

And now he was asking me if I wanted a veggie burger. Do guys generally ask their girlfriends if they want a veggie burger right before they break up with them? I wasn't very well versed in these matters, so the truth was, I didn't know.

But I didn't think so.

"Um," I said, intelligently. "I don't know." I thought maybe it was a trick question. "If you're having one, I guess."

So then Michael went, "Okay," and gestured for me to follow him, and we went into the kitchen, where Lilly was sitting, using the granite countertop to lay out her storyboards for the episode of *Lilly Tells It Like It Is* she was filming the next day.

"Jeez," she said, when she saw me. "What happened to you? You look like you swapped outfits with the Sugar Plum Fairy."

"I was at a ball," I reminded her.

"Oh, yeah," Lilly said. "Well, if you ask me, the Sugar Plum Fairy got the better deal. But I'm not supposed to be here. So don't mind me."

"We won't," Michael assured her.

And then he did the strangest thing. He started to cook.

Seriously. He was *cooking*.

Well, okay, not really cooking, more like reheating. Still, he fully got out these two veggie burgers he'd gotten from Balducci's, and put them on some buns, and then put the buns on these two plates. And then he took some fries that had been in the oven on a tray and put them onto the two plates, as well. And then he got ketchup and mayo and mustard out of the fridge, along with two cans of Coke, and he put all that stuff on a tray, and then he walked out of the kitchen, and before

I could ask Lilly what in the name of all that was holy was going on, he came back, picked up the two plates, and went, to me, "Come on."

What could I do, but follow him?

I trailed after him into the TV room, where Lilly and I had viewed so many cinematic gems for the first time, such as *Valley Girl* and *Bring It On* and *Attack of the 50 Foot Woman* and *Crossing Delancey*.

And there, in front of the Moscovitzes' black leather couch, which sat in front of their thirty-two-inch Sony TV, sat two little folding tables. Michael lowered the plates of food he'd prepared onto them. They sat there, in the glow of the *Star Wars* title image, which was frozen on the TV screen, obviously paused there.

"Michael," I said, genuinely baffled. "What *is* this?"

"Well, you couldn't make it to the Screening Room," he said, looking as if he couldn't quite believe I hadn't figured it out on my own yet. "So I brought the Screening Room to you. Come on, let's eat. I'm starved."

He might have been starved, but I was stunned. I stood there looking down at the veggie burgers—which smelled divine—going, "Wait a minute. Wait a minute. You aren't breaking up with me?"

Michael had already sat down on the couch and stuffed a few fries in his mouth. When I said that, about breaking up, he turned around to look at me like

I was demented. "Break up with you? Why would I do that?"

"Well," I said, starting to wonder if maybe he was right, and I really *was* demented. "When I told you I couldn't make it tonight you . . . well, you seemed kind of distant—"

"I wasn't distant," Michael said. "I was trying to figure out what we could do instead of, you know, going to the movie."

"But then you didn't show up for lunch. . . ."

"Right," Michael said. "I had to call and order the veggie burgers and beg Maya to go to the store and get the rest of the stuff. And my dad had loaned our *Star Wars* DVD to a friend of his, so I had to call him and make him get it back."

I listened in astonishment. Everyone, it seemed—Maya, the Moscovitzes' housekeeper; Lilly; even Michael's parents—had been in on Michael's scheme to recreate the Screening Room right in his own apartment.

Only I had been in ignorance of his plan. Just as he had been in ignorance of my belief that he was about to break up with me.

"Oh," I said, beginning to feel like the world's number-one dork. "So . . . you don't want to break up?"

"No, I don't want to break up," Michael said, starting to look mad now—probably the way Mr. Rochester looked when he heard Jane had been hanging out with that St. John guy. "Mia, I love you, remember? Why would I want to break up with you? Now come sit down and eat before it gets cold."

Then I wasn't *beginning* to feel like the world's number-one dork: I *totally* felt like it.

But at the same time, I felt incredibly, blissfully happy. Because Michael had said the L word! Said it right to my face! And in a very bossy way, just like Captain von Trapp or the Beast or Patrick Swayze!

Then Michael hit the play button on the remote, and the first chords of John Williams's brilliant *Star Wars* theme filled the room. And Michael went, "Mia, come on. Unless you want to change out of that dress first. Did you bring any normal clothes?"

Still, something wasn't right. Not completely.

"Do you just love me like a friend?" I asked him, trying to sound cynically amused, you know, the way René would, in order to keep the truth from him—that my heart was pounding a mile a minute. "Or are you *in* love with me?"

Michael was staring over the back of the couch at me. He looked like he couldn't quite believe his ears. I couldn't believe my own. Had I really just asked him that? Just come out and asked him, flying in the face of all Tina and I had discussed?

Apparently—judging from his incredulous expression, anyway—I had. I could feel myself starting to turn redder, and redder, and redder, and redder. . . .

Jane Eyre would so never have asked that question.

But then again, maybe she ought to have. Because the way Michael responded made the whole embarrassment of having had to ask completely and totally worth it. And the way he responded was, he reached out, took the tiara from me, laid it down on the couch beside him, took both my hands in his, pulled me toward him, and gave me a really long kiss.

On the lips.

Of the French variety.

We missed the entire scrolling prologue to the movie, due to kissing. Then finally when the sound of Princess Leia's starship being fired upon roused us from our passionate embrace, Michael said, "Of course I'm in love with you. Now come sit down and eat."

It truly was the most romantic moment of my entire life. If I live to be as old as Grandmère, I will never be as happy as I was at that moment. I just stood there, thrilled to pieces, for about a minute. I mean, I could barely get over it. He loved me. Not only that, he was *in* love with me! Michael Moscovitz is in love with me, Mia Thermopolis!

"Your burger is getting cold," he said.

See? See how perfect we are for each other? He is so practical, while I have my head in the clouds. Has there ever been as perfect a couple? Has there ever been as perfect a date?

We sat there, eating our veggie burgers and watching

Star Wars, he in his jeans and vintage Boomtown Rats T-shirt, and me in my Chanel ball gown. And when Ben Kenobi said, "Obi-Wan? That's a name I haven't heard in a long time," we both went, right on cue, "How long?" And Ben said, as he always does, "A very long time."

And when, just before Luke flies off to attack the Death Star, Michael put it on pause so he could go get dessert, I helped him clear the plates.

And then, while he was making the ice-cream sundaes, I snuck back into the TV room, and put his present on his TV table, and waited for him to come back and find it, which he did, a few minutes later.

"What's this?" he wanted to know, as he handed me my sundae, vanilla ice cream drowning in a sea of hot fudge, whipped cream, and pistachios.

"It's your birthday present," I said, barely able to contain myself, I was so excited to see what he'd think of it. It was way better than candy or a sweater. It was, I thought, the perfect gift for Michael.

I feel like I had a right to be excited, because I'd paid a pretty hefty price for Michael's gift . . . weeks of worrying about being found out, and then, after having been found out, being forced to waltz with Prince René, who was a good dancer, and all, but who kind of smelled like an ashtray, to tell the truth.

So I was pretty stoked as Michael, with a puzzled expression on his face, sat down and picked up the box.

"I told you that you didn't have to get me anything," he said.

"I know." I was bouncing up and down, I was so excited. "But I wanted to. And I saw this, and I thought it was *perfect*."

"Well," Michael said. "Thanks." He untied the ribbon that held the minuscule box closed, then lifted the lid. . . .

And there, sitting on a wad of white cotton, it was. A dirty little rock, no bigger than an ant. Smaller than an ant, even. The size of the head of a pushpin.

"Huh," Michael said, looking down at the tiny speck. "It's . . . it's really nice."

I laughed delightedly. "You don't even know what it is!"

"Well," he said. "No, I don't."

"Can't you guess?"

"Well," he said, again. "It looks like . . . I mean, it closely resembles . . . a rock."

"It *is* a rock," I said. "Guess where it's from."

Michael eyed the rock. "I don't know. Genovia?"

"No, silly," I crowed. "The moon! It's a moon rock! From when Neil Armstrong was up there. He collected a bunch of them, and then brought them back and gave them to the White House, and Richard Nixon gave my grandmother a bunch of them when he was in office. Well, he gave them to Genovia, technically. And I saw them and thought . . . well, that you should have one. Because I know you like space stuff. I mean how you've got the glow-in-the-dark constellations on the ceiling over your bed and all . . ."

Michael looked up from the moon rock—which he'd been staring down at like he couldn't quite believe what he was seeing—and went, "When were you in my room?"

"Oh," I said, feeling myself beginning to blush again. "A long time ago—" Well, it *had* been a long time ago. It had been way back before I'd known he liked me, when I'd been sending him those anonymous love poems "—once when Maya was cleaning in there."

Michael said, "Oh," and looked back down at the moon rock.

"Mia," he said, a few seconds later. "I can't accept this."

"Yes, you can," I said. "There's plenty left back at the palace museum, don't worry. Richard Nixon must have really had a thing for Grandmère, because I'm pretty sure we got more moon rocks than Monaco or anybody else. "

"Mia," Michael said. "It's a rock. From the *moon*."

"Right," I said, not certain what he was getting at. Did he not like it? It *was* kind of weird, I guess, to give your boyfriend a rock for his birthday. But it wasn't just any rock. And Michael wasn't just any boyfriend. I'd really thought he'd like it.

"It's a rock," he said again, "that came from two

hundred thirty thousand miles away. From Earth. Two hundred thirty thousand miles away from Earth."

"Yes," I said, wondering what I had done wrong. I had only just gotten Michael back, after having spent a whole week convinced he was going to dump me over one thing, only to discover that he was going to dump me over something else entirely? There is seriously no justice in the world. "Michael, if you don't like it, I can give it back. I just thought—"

"No way," he said, moving the box out of my grasp. "You're not getting this back. I just don't know what I'm going to get you for your birthday. This is going to be a hard act to follow."

Was that all? I felt my blush receding.

"Oh, that," I said. "You can just write me another song."

Which was kind of vixenish of me to say, because he had never admitted that the song, the first one he'd ever played me, "Tall Drink of Water," was about me. But I could tell by the way he was smiling now that I'd guessed correctly. It was. It *totally* was.

So then we ate our sundaes and watched the rest of the movie, and when it was over and the credits were rolling, I remembered something else I'd meant to give him, something I'd thought of in the cab on the way down from the Contessa's, when I'd been trying to think up what I was going to say to him if he broke up with me.

"Oh," I said. "I thought of a name for your band."

"Not," he said with a groan, "the X-Wing Fighters. I beg of you."

"No," I said. "Skinner Box." Which is this thing this one psychologist used on all these rats and pigeons to prove there's such a thing as a conditioned response. Pavlov, the guy Michael had named his dog after, had done the same thing, but with dogs and bells.

"Skinner Box," Michael said carefully.

"Yeah," I said. "I mean, I just figured, since you named your dog Pavlov—"

"I kind of like it," Michael said. "I'll see what the guys say."

I beamed. The evening was turning out so much better than I had originally thought it would, I couldn't really do anything *but* beam. In fact, that's why I locked myself in the bathroom. To try to calm down a little. I am so happy, I can barely write. I—

Saturday, January 24, the loft

Oops. I had to break off there last night, because Lilly started banging on the bathroom door, wanting to know whether I'd suddenly become bulimic or something. When I opened it (the door, I mean) and she saw me in there with my journal and my pen, and she went, all crabby (Lilly is more of a morning person than a night person), "Do you mean to say you've been in here for the past half hour *writing in your journal*?"

Which I'll admit is a little weird, but I couldn't help it. I was so happy, I HAD to write it down, so I would never forget how it felt.

"And you *still* haven't figured out what you're good at?" she asked.

When I shook my head, she just stomped away, all mad.

But I couldn't be annoyed with her, because . . . well, because I'm so in love with her brother.

The same way I can't really be mad at Grandmère, even though she did, in essence, try to foist me off on this homeless prince last night. But I can't blame her for trying. She was only trying to make herself look better in front of her friend.

Besides, she called here a little while ago, wanting to know if I was feeling all right after the bad truffle I'd ingested. My mom, playing along, assured her that I was fine. So then Grandmère wanted to know if I could come over and have tea with her and the Contessa . . . who was just dying to get to know me better. I said I was busy with homework. Which ought to impress the Contessa. You know, with my diligent work ethic.

And I can't be mad at René, either, after the way he fully came to my aid last night. I wonder how he and Bella got along. It would be pretty funny if they hit it off . . . well, funny to everyone but Grandmère.

And I can't even be mad at Thompson Street Cleaners for losing my Queen Amidala underwear, because this morning there was a knock on the door to the loft, and when I opened it, our neighbor Ronnie was there with a big bag of our laundry, including Mr. G's brown cords and my mom's Free Winona T-shirt. Ronnie says she must have accidentally picked up the wrong bag from the vestibule, and then she'd gone to Barbados with her boss for the holidays, and only just now noticed that she had a bag of clothing that was not her own.

Although I am not as happy about getting my Queen Amidala underwear back as you might think. Because clearly, I can get along without them. I was thinking about asking for more of them for my birthday, but now I don't have to, because Michael, even though he doesn't know it, has already given me the greatest gift I've ever gotten.

And no, it's not his love—although that is probably the second greatest thing he could have given me. No, it's something that he said after Lilly went stomping away from the bathroom.

"What was that all about?" he wanted to know.

"Oh," I said, putting away my journal, "she's just mad because I haven't figured out what my secret talent is."

"Your what?" Michael said.

"My secret talent." And then, because he'd been so honest with me, with the whole being in love thing, I decided to be honest with him, too. So I explained, "It's just that you and Lilly, you're both so talented. You guys are good at so many things, and I'm not good at anything, and sometimes I feel like . . . well, like I don't belong. At least not in Gifted and Talented class, anyway."

"Mia," Michael said. "You're totally gifted."

"Yeah," I said, fingering my dress. "At looking like a snowdrop."

"No," Michael said. "Although now that you mention it, you're pretty good at that, too. But I meant writing."

I have to admit, I kind of stared at him, and went, in a pretty unprincesslike manner, "Huh?"

"Well, it's pretty obvious," he said, "that you like to write. I mean, your head is always buried in that journal. And you always get A's on your papers in English. I think it's pretty obvious, Mia, that you're a writer."

And even though I had never really thought about

it before, I realized Michael was right. I mean, I *am* always writing in this journal. And I do compose a lot of poetry, and write a lot of notes and e-mails and stuff. I mean, I feel like I am *always* writing. I do it so much, I never even thought about it as being a *talent*. It's just something I do all the time, like breathing.

But now that I know what my talent is, you can bet I am going to start working on honing it. And the first thing I'm going to write is a bill to submit before the Genovian Parliament to get some traffic lights downtown. The intersections there are *murder*. . . .

Right after I get home from going bowling with Michael and Lilly and Boris. Because even a princess has to have fun sometimes.

For all the books about Mia and more by
MEG CABOT
check out the following pages!

You'll find:

- An excerpt from the fifth Princess Diaries
  book, *Princess in Pink*
- More about the rest of the Princess Diaries
  series
- A detailed list of Meg's other exciting books

Still not enough?
For even more about Meg Cabot, go to:

•

www.megcabot.com

You can read Meg's online diary,
find the latest info on her books,
take quizzes, and get advice on how to
handle the paparazzi.

THE ATOM

The Official Student-Run Newspaper of Albert Einstein High School
Take Pride in the AEHS Lions

Week of May 5   Volume 456/Issue 27

Science Fair Winners Announced
by Rafael Menendez

Science students entered 21 projects in the Albert Einstein High School Science Fair. Several projects advanced to the New York City regional competition, which will be held next month. Senior Judith Gershner received the grand prize for slicing a human genome. Earning special honors were senior Michael Moscovitz for his computer program modeling the death of a dwarf star, and freshman Kenneth Showalter for his experiments in gender transfiguration in newts.

Lacrosse Teams Win
by Ai-Lin Hong

Both the varsity and junior varsity lacrosse teams beat their competitors this past weekend. Senior Josh Richter led the varsity team to a stunning defeat of the Dwight School 7–6 in overtime. The JV team defeated Dwight by a score of 8–0. The exciting games were marred by a peculiarly aggressive Central Park squirrel that continuously darted out onto the field. Eventually it was chased away by Principal Gupta.

AEHS's Princess Spends Spring Break Building Homes for Appalachian Poor
by Melanie Greenbaum

Spring break was a working holiday for AEHS freshman Mia Thermopolis. Mia, who, it was revealed last fall is actually the sole heir to the throne of the principality of Genovia, spent her five-day vacation helping build homes for Housing for the Hopeful. Said the princess of her sojourn into the foothills of the Smokey Mountains, building two-bedroom homes for the underprivileged: "It was okay. Except for the whole no bathroom thing. And the part where I kept hitting myself in the thumb with my hammer."

Senior Week
by Josh Richter,
senior class president

The week of May 5–May 10 is Senior Week. This is the time to honor this year's AEHS graduating class, who has worked so hard to show you leadership throughout the year. The Senior Week Events Calendar goes like this:

Mon:
Senior Awards Banquet

Tues:
Senior Sports Banquet

Wed:
Senior Debate

Thurs:
Senior Skit Nite

Fri:
Senior Skip Day

Sat:
Senior Prom

A Note From Your Principal:

Senior Skip Day is not an event sanctioned by school administration. All students are required to attend classes Friday, May 9. In addition, the request made by certain members of the freshman class to lift the sanction against underclassmen attending the prom unless invited by an upperclassman is denied.

Notice to All Students:

It has come to the attention of the administration that many pupils do not seem to know the proper words to the AEHS school song. They are as follows:

Einstein Lions, we're for you
Come on, be bold, come on,
be bold, come on, be bold
Einstein Lions, we're for you
Blue and gold, blue
and gold, blue and gold
Einstein Lions, we're for you
We've got a team no one
else can ever tame
Einstein Lions, we're for you
Let's win this game!

Please note that at this year's graduation ceremony, any student caught singing alternative (particularly explicit and/or suggestive) words to the AEHS school song will be removed from the premises. Complaints that the AEHS school song is too militaristic must be submitted in writing to the AEHS administrative office, not scrawled on bathroom door stalls or discussed on any student's public access television program.

Letters to the Editor:

To Whom it May Concern: Melanie Greenbaum's article in last week's issue of the *Atom* on the strides the women's movement has made in the past three decades was laughably facile. Sexism is still alive and well, not only around the world, but in our own country. In Utah, for instance, polygamous marriages involving brides as young as 11 years of age are thriving, practiced by fundamentalist Mormons who continue to live by traditions their ancestors brought west in the mid-1800s. The number of people in polygamous families in Utah is estimated by human rights groups at perhaps as many as 50,000, despite the fact that polygamy is not tolerated by the mainstream Mormon church, and the enactment of tough penalties in the case of underage brides that can sentence a polygamous husband or church leader arranging such a marriage to up to 15 years in prison.

I am not telling other cultures how to live, or anything. I am just saying take off the rose-colored glasses, Ms. Greenbaum, and write an article about some of the real problems that affect half the population of this planet. The staff of the *Atom* might well consider giving some of their other writers a chance to report on these issues, instead of relegating them to the cafeteria beat.

—Lilly Moscovitz

AEHS Food Court Menu
compiled by Mia Thermopolis

Mon. Potato Bar, Fr. Bread Pizza, Fish Fingers, Meatball Sub, Spicy Chix

Tues. Soup & Sand, Chicken Patty, Tuna in Pita, Indiv. Pizza, Nachos Deluxe

Wed. Taco Salad Bar, Burrito, Corndog/Pickle, Deli Bar, Italian Beef

Thurs. Asian Bar, Chicken Parm, Corn/FF Pasta Bar, Fish Stix

Fri. Bean Bar, Grilled Cheese, Curley Fries, Buffalo Bites, Soft Pretzel

Reward for safe return. Locker #510

Happy ad
Happy Birthday in advance, MT!
Love,
Your Loyal Subjects

Happy ad
Shop at Ho's Deli for all your school supply needs! New this week: erasers, staples, notebooks, pens. Also Yu-Gi-Oh cards/Slim-fast in Strawberry.

For Sale:
One Fender precision bass, baby blue, never been played. With amp, how-to videos. $300. Locker #345

Looking for Love:
Female frosh, loves romance/reading, wants older boy who enjoys same. Must be taller than 5'8", no mean people, nonsmokers only. NO METALHEADS.
E-mail: Iluvromance@aehs.edu

Happy ad
Personal to MK from MW:
My love for you
Like a flower grows
Where it will stop
No one knows.

Wednesday, April 30, Bio

Mia, did you see the latest issue of the Atom?—Shameeka

I know, I just got my copy. I wish Lilly would stop mentioning me in her letters to the editor. I mean, as the only freshman on the newspaper staff, I have to pay my dues. Leslie Cho, the editor-in-chief, got her start on the cafeteria beat. I am TOTALLY FINE with covering the lunch menu every week.

Well, I think Lilly just feels if your goal really is to be a writer someday, you aren't going to get there writing about Buffalo Bites!

That is not true. I have made some very important innovations in the lunch column. For instance, it was my idea to capitalize the *I* in *Individual Pizza*.

Lilly is only looking out for your best interests.

Whatever. Melanie Greenbaum is on the girls' basketball team. She could fully slam dunk me if she wanted to. I don't think Lilly antagonizing her is in my best interest.

So . . .

So what?

So has he asked you yet?????

Has who asked me what?

*HAS MICHAEL ASKED YOU TO THE
PROM???????*

Oh. No.

*Mia, the prom is in less than TWO WEEKS! Jeff asked
me a MONTH ago. How are you going to get your dress
in time if you don't find out soon whether or not you're
going? Plus you have to make an appointment to get your
hair and nails done, and get the boutonniere, and he has to
rent the limo and his tux and make dinner reservations. This
is not pizza at Bowlmor Lanes, you know. It's dinner and
dancing at Maxim's! It's serious!*

I'm sure Michael is going to ask me soon. He has a
lot on his mind, what with the new band and college
in the fall and all.

*Well, you better light a fire under him. Because you don't
want to end up having him ask at the last minute. Because
then if you say yes it'll be like you were waiting around for
him to ask.*

Hello, Michael and I are going out. It's not like I'm going to go with somebody else. As if anybody else would ask me. I mean, I'm not YOU, Shameeka. I don't have all these senior guys lined up at my locker, just waiting for a chance to ask me out. Not that I would. Go out with another guy, I mean. If one asked. Because I love Michael with every fiber of my being.

Well, I hope he asks you soon, because I don't want to be the only freshman girl at the prom! Who will I hang with in the ladies' room?

Don't worry. I'll be there. Oops. What was that about ice worms?

They differ from earthworms in that they_____

READ ALL THE BOOKS ABOUT MIA:

The Princess Diaries

Mia learns she is a princess, receives her first kiss,
and is equally befuddled by both.

THE PRINCESS DIARIES, VOLUME II:
Princess in the Spotlight

Mia has a wedding to plan (not hers!), a visiting
cousin on the loose, and best of all, a secret admirer.

THE PRINCESS DIARIES, VOLUME III:
Princess in Love

Mia's starting to get the hang of her
newfound royalty, but she still can't get her
prince charming . . . or can she?

THE PRINCESS DIARIES, VOLUME IV:
Princess in Waiting

Meeting the Genovian subjects is one thing,
but planning a first date is quite another!
Isn't there anything Mia is good at besides
inheriting an unwanted royal title?

THE PRINCESS DIARIES, VOLUME IV AND A HALF:
Project Princess

Mia divides spring break between building a
house for the underprivileged and making out with
Michael. What could be more fun?

THE PRINCESS DIARIES, VOLUME V:
Princess in Pink

With Lilly and Grandmère on opposite sides
of a service workers strike, Mia must do
something to prevent the prom from being
cancelled AND get Michael to take her to it!

THE PRINCESS DIARIES, VOLUME VI:
Princess in Training

Between her evil English teacher, school
president elections, and a Genovian eco-crisis, can
Mia handle sophomore Geometry—or having
a boyfriend who's in college?

The Princess Present
A PRINCESS DIARIES BOOK

In this charming novella, Mia visits Genovia for
the holidays and worries about her present for
Michael. What she doesn't realize is that what makes
a present perfect has nothing to do with international
express courier, and everything to do with love.
Though some shiny ribbon never hurts.

A Princess Diaries Book

Yes! Finally!
Just what you've been waiting for!
This book has it all:

- Preventing your tiara from slipping off
- Keeping your pores squeaky clean
- Winning the heart of the boy of your dreams (or, at the very least, the cute guy you sit next to in language lab)
- Avoiding a military incursion by a neighboring principality
- And much, much more!

By following the invaluable advice of Mia and her very special guest authors (including best friend and urban guerrilla Lilly Moscovitz; Grandmère, the dowager princess of Genovia; Manhattan beauty expert Paolo; Italian fashion specialist Sebastiano Grimaldi; and Tina Hakim Baba, resident high school romance expert), you will be well prepared for the day you finally ascend the throne . . . or at the very least, you'll know the difference between a fish fork and a salad fork.

Perfect Princess

A Princess Diaries Book

Do you know . . .

- ➤ How to wield the incredible power of the tiara?
- ➤ When your prince deserves to be whacked in the head with a shoe?
- ➤ What it takes to achieve immortality . . . or at least make an unforgettable entrance?
- ➤ Why allowing the populace to eat bread and not just cake is of critical importance?
- ➤ What to do as a houseguest should you find a pea under your mattress?
- ➤ What makes a princess perfect?

Princess Amelia Mignonette Grimaldi Thermopolis Renaldo of Genovia (aka Mia) and subjects look to the world's princesses for the answers to these burning questions and more. Big and small, old and new, real and imaginary—all kinds of princesses exhibit perfection in their own way. Don't delay: Find out what made this royal roster rule, and begin your own reign!

Girl-next-door Jenny Greenley goes stir-crazy
(or star-crazy?)
in Meg Cabot's

*Ask Annie your most complex interpersonal
relationship questions. Go on, we dare you!*

*All letters to Annie are subject to publi-
cation in the Clayton High School Register.
Names and e-mail addresses of correspondents
guaranteed confidential.*

High school junior Jenny Greenley is good at solving problems . . . so good she's the school newspaper's anonymous
advice columnist. Even if solving other people's problems
doesn't make her own—like not having a boyfriend—go
away, it's still fun. But when nineteen-year-old screen sensation Luke Striker comes to Jen's small town to research a
role, he creates havoc that even levelheaded Jenny isn't sure
she can repair . . . especially since she's right in the middle
of it.

Can Jen, who always manages to be there for everybody
else, learn to take her own advice, and find true love at last?

Samantha Madison saves the day!
(sort of)
in Meg Cabot's

ALL-AMERICAN GIRL

Top ten reasons Samantha Madison is in deep trouble:

10. Her big sister is the most popular girl in school
9. Her little sister is a certified genius
8. She's in love with her big sister's boyfriend
7. She got caught selling celebrity portraits in school
6. And now she's being forced to take art classes
5. She's just saved the president of the United States from an assassination attempt
4. So the whole world thinks she's a hero
3. Even though Sam knows she is far, far from being a hero
2. And now she's been appointed teen ambassador to the UN

And the number-one reason Sam's life is over?

1. The president's son might just be in love with her

the mediator

Mia Thermopolis is a princess, Jenny Greenley is a tabloid target, and Samantha Madison is a national heroine, but Susannah Simon is an altogether different kind of girl. The star of Meg Cabot's Mediator series, Suze can see ghosts. Which is kind of a pain most of the time, but when Suze moves to California and finds Jesse, the ghost of a nineteenth-century hottie haunting her bedroom, things begin to look up.

THE MEDIATOR 1:
Shadowland

There's a hot guy in Susannah Simon's bedroom. Too bad he's a ghost.

THE MEDIATOR 2:
Ninth Key

Tad Beaumont, totally dreamy, has actually asked Suze out on a date! But ghosts tend to ruin everything. Especially your love life.

THE MEDIATOR 3:
Reunion

The ghosts of four teenagers who were in a terrible car accident are haunting Susannah. But accidents happen. Or do they?

THE MEDIATOR 4:
Darkest Hour

What—or who—is buried in Susannah's backyard? The ghost of Maria de Silva, Jesse's fiancée before his murder, may have the answers. But does Suze really want to know?

THE MEDIATOR 5:
Haunted

Paul's the only other mediator Suze has ever met—and he's actually kinda cute. So why does he give her the chills? Is it possible to be haunted by someone who isn't even dead?

THE MEDIATOR 6:
Twilight

Paul has ideas of his own, and they involve sending Jesse to the Great Beyond. For good. But will Jesse choose to live without Susannah, or die to love her?

Finally, don't miss these two irresistible
love stories by Meg Cabot.
All the fun of *The Princess Diaries*,
with a Jane Austen twist!

NICOLA AND THE VISCOUNT

It's only her first London Season, but sixteen-year-old
Nicola has made up her mind: handsome, charming,
poetry-reading Lord Sebastian is, simply, a god. So
when the divine viscount starts paying special attention
to her, Nicola is certain she's found her destiny.

Everything is perfect until the infuriating—and dis-
turbingly handsome—Nathaniel Sheridan begins to
cast doubt on the viscount's character . . . and on
Nicola's feelings.

VICTORIA AND THE ROGUE

Wealthy young heiress Lady Victoria Arbuthnot is
accustomed to handling her own affairs—and everyone
else's. So when she's suddenly sent to London to find a
husband, Victoria quickly finds a perfect English
gentleman.

Everything is just as she wants it—that is, if the
raffish young ship captain Jacob Carstairs would stop
meddling with her plans.